LI V E D

Life

LIVED *Life*

THE COUNTER DOUBLE BLUFF

DAMOND DAVIS

Preface

What would you do if you had only ten days to live? Would you reflect on how great things were? Are? Could have been? My name is—well, my name isn't important, and we don't have much time anyway. I'm about to tell you the best and worst stories I've ever heard, lived, and shared. These stories are meant to add value to your experiences and hopefully give you something to draw strength from as you navigate life. Some of them may entertain you, some may speak to your deepest emotions; either way, this is lived life. The language is real, the people are authentic, and their stories are a captivating and genuine depiction of life's mistakes and delectable passions. I want you to know that you are not alone, and many of the people in these stories, just like you, didn't stop where they started. They continued to progress and mature as a result of lived life.

I've always been the person who kept everyone's secrets, and up until now, I've never spoken these truths. The names have been changed to protect the points of view. The setting is the small town of Cadensville, California, a place that's far away from everyday life yet close enough to Las Vegas to get its fair share of visitors.

Please enjoy. Read with empathy, fear, and love, and find hope in the reality of lived life.

Two years earlier...

Candis

I t was the annual Christmas Gala at the grand ballroom in the Hilton on West Street in downtown Los Angeles. As long as Candis could remember, they'd always held it there. She walked in by herself and made her way to the elevator bank. The operator greeted her, and if you've ever been to this Hilton, you'll know who I'm talking about. He's a big man with an even bigger presence—quick with his wit, always finds a way to brighten your day. He probably was, or should have been, a comedian. Perhaps even an actor.

"How are you tonight, Madam?" he asked Candis, admiring her coat. Even if you didn't know it was an in-season Loro Piana coat, you knew it was money. The subtle design and deep aubergine were stunning. Its matching dyed mink collar screamed, "I have money and I'm not afraid to spend it." It wasn't so bold for the office as to induce a frown from the self-appointed "clothing police," but it showed just the right amount of leg when she stepped out in the evenings. Not that any of that mattered to Candis. No, the best thing about the coat was that it was a gift—from him.

As her thoughts drifted to him, the operator interrupted: "Ma'am?"

Candis quietly, almost hesitantly, replied, "Hmmm?"

At work, she had all the confidence in the world. Outside the office, she was shy, quiet, reserved. She always thought people were looking at her skin. She was too dark, she thought, and it made her especially self-conscious. It had been that way since elementary school. It was something she'd never gotten over, and she'd given up thinking she could shake it. She was clever, pretty, and always put together, yet she never felt quite like she measured up.

"Ma'am, I said it's cold out there. There's no reason for it to be that cold in here."

"I'm sorry, sir, you're right," she said with a smile. "It's been a long day." And with genuine warmth, she wished him and his family happy holidays. He smiled in return, then the elevator stopped, and with a slight nod, he opened the door.

"We're here, Ma'am. Now you keep smiling and have a wonderful time at the party."

That wouldn't be a problem. The party was *always* a good time; it was nothing to see senators, ballplayers, and celebrities. People started angling for invitations six months in advance.

She spotted Linda as soon as she stepped into the party. Everyone's eyes naturally found Linda. She was one of the most beautiful women in LA: dyed blond hair, fair skin, a striking resemblance to Vanessa Williams (they had the same build, voice, and eyes). Everyone loved her, and she seemed to love everyone. An extremely intelligent woman, she possessed a lethal combination of beauty and brains. No boardroom stood a chance once she walked through the door. The CEO called her the "closer." She had been with the company since she graduated from college and helped build it into a Fortune 100 consulting firm. She'd brought in over $200 million in business over the last five quarters.

When her husband was killed in Iraq, she took the life insurance money and set up a foundation in his name. Her grief was unrelenting, but she tried to combat it by staying busy—volunteering at shelters and Habitat for Humanity, teaching fitness classes, running marathons about every other month. Tonight, she had a surprise announcement to make, and the party was already buzzing with anticipation.

"Hey girl!" Linda yelled when she spotted Candis hurrying over to embrace her.

"Hey! How are you? Nervous? I'm so excited!"

"Yes, honey," Linda said. "I may be ready to hang up my cleats. This game is for you young runners." Linda always made reference to her days as a track runner back at Riverside High School. She still held several titles but was now living vicariously through her son, who ran track in college.

"What would this company do without you?" Candis said. "I've learned so much from you and feel so fortunate to have you as my mentor."

Candis's eyes began to well with tears, and as soon as Linda saw the emotion rising, her hand went to Candis's arm and she said, "Look, I'm not dying, girl. This ain't my funeral, so be cool."

"Okay, I know," Candis said, fighting back the tears and forcing a smile. "I'm getting myself a drink. You want something?"

"Naw, girl, I'm good. I don't need to be drunk for my speech."

Linda was quickly absorbed into a group of partygoers as Candis walked off toward the bar.

Linda's son Justin was working the bar. He wasn't technically a bartender, but he'd mixed enough drinks in his college years to know what he was doing. He had an app on his phone for the more difficult drinks. He would do anything for his mom, including work the bar for free on a night when he could be hanging with his guys. Candis loved the bond he had with Linda.

"Hey, Candis, I haven't seen you since the last party. How are you?"

"I'm good, baby. Now go ahead and fix up my drink. I'll take a Cosmopolitan." Just as she was ordering, she heard a voice behind her say, "You look stunning, Candis."

It was Kevin. She knew it without even turning around. She rolled her eyes slightly. He often annoyed her; it was like he was always trying way too hard. "Oh, hi Kevin," she said over her shoulder. "Thanks."

Kevin was a nice, hardworking young man, kind of round in the Al Roker way, but handsome. He looked like he'd played football in high school or college but let work get in the way of the gym. He was Linda's assistant before his promotion to junior consultant. His father had passed away a year before his promotion, and his mom was in the early stages of cancer. Kevin was such a kindhearted guy that he'd moved in to care for her and help with the treatments. In Linda's eyes, and in the eyes of everyone else in the company, he and Candis were the perfect match. But the man boobs peeking through his shirt gave Candis pause.

Besides, she had her mind on another man. Nobody else stood a chance.

"Coming right up!" Justin said before Kevin could say another word. He set to work making her drink.

She smiled at the save and leaned her elbows on the bar as Kevin walked off. "Have a good night, Kevin!" she called lightly, with relief. "Thanks, Justin. That was a close one!"

They both laughed, and she continued, "Okay, you're not off the hook yet, buddy. Give me updates. How's school?"

"I'm still finishing up this business degree and running track. It's nice, and I feel like I understand it much better than I did last year. I appreciate all of your help breaking down economics."

"Hey, no worries. That stuff comes easy to me. I'm just happy you're working it out and are ready to come out soon. What—next year?"

"That's right!" Justin said with a smile. A few more thirsty customers walked up to the bar.

Justin wanted to head Candis off before she headed down the girlfriend path, but before he could greet the new faces, she said with a big-sisterly smirk, "Okay, how about girls?"

He smiled sheepishly. "Come on, now. You already know I don't have anyone serious, but there are a few young ladies who have caught my eye."

"That's right, baby," she said. "You don't rush into anything."

"I know. My mom has been preaching the same thing." He slid her drink across the bar with a smile. "Here's your Cosmo. Let me know if it works for you."

Candis took one sip and said, "Perfect, thanks baby. I'll see you for another one of these in a little bit." She winked and then walked over to the table where Lance, the company's custodian, was sitting with a woman Candis assumed was his girlfriend. She was beautiful—wearing the hell out of a gorgeous red dress that had to be a Carolina Herrera. Candis needed to get a look at the shoes to see if this girl really knew how to slay an event. Candis got a little closer and looked down. To her surprise, the woman's feet were adorned with the exact pair of Jimmy Choos Candis was wearing.

"I know Lance can't afford those kind of shoes," Candis thought.

"Cute shoes, girl!" Candice said out loud, smiling at Lance and lifting a foot for the woman to see.

"Great minds think alike!"

They shared a laugh, then Lance introduced Candis to Sydney. The ladies talked for a while, exchanging pleasantries.

Candis reminded Lance that he should definitely take a load off and take advantage of the open bar.

"Indeed!" Lance said. "They be working me like a Hebrew slave. I came to enjoy myself."

Candis laughed again and soon after was off to greet more people on the other side of the room.

There were brightly lit wreaths on the streetlights and telephone poles outside, blurred by a haze of condensation on the windows. People were still showing up even after Candis got there, and she was an hour late. She felt her phone buzz in her purse and checked the screen. It was *him*. She answered with excitement. "Hello?"

"Hey, baby. What's happenin'?" He always greeted her that way, and she loved it. "I'm his baby," she thought. It made her feel like the most special person in the world.

"Will you come downstairs for a minute?" he asked.

"Wait. You're here? What?" She was so excited, she immediately put down her drink and hurried toward the elevator. It was just opening—perfect timing.

The elevator operator noted her smile and couldn't help but comment. "Oh, I get it now. You going to see *him*, ain't you?"

She tried to frown but smiled instead as she mustered, "Mind ya bidnezz, sir! You don't know my life." They both grinned.

"Darling, I have worked this elevator a long time, and I know exactly where you're headed. Your body language is telling on you." He laughed. When they reached the bottom, he said, "You have a good night now."

"Oh, I'll be back," she said.

"No you won't." His eyes sparkled. "You just don't know it yet."

He couldn't have been more right. Her man had come to town and reserved a room at the hotel where the gala was happening. It all made sense now. The week prior they'd been on the phone, and he was persistent in asking about the Christmas Gala because he was trying to plan but didn't want to tip his hand. Candis said it would be great if he made it, even though he was gone on business and she assumed there was no way he could. He traveled *a lot* for work, making him a platinum or medallion member on just about every reward card he owned. But he slid into town undetected and was just waiting for the right time to surprise her.

They met in the lobby, and when he passed her the key, she immediately felt the need to move this party to the room—never mind the Gala. She grabbed his arm and, barely saying a word, took him right upstairs. She was just starting to take off his clothes when her phone buzzed.

It was Kevin, texting to find out where she was because Linda was about to speak, but Candis was preoccupied now. She was about to reach heaven. Nothing else mattered. By the time her phone stopped buzzing, she had succeeded in undressing him down to his socks—he removed those himself, then returned the favor, slowly taking off her Badgley Mischka designer gown. She wanted him to move a little faster. She needed him to move a lot faster. She had waited weeks to be this close to him again. He knew she wanted him, so he teased her, stopping to kiss her back after removing only the straps of her gown. Candis couldn't take it anymore. She spun on her heels and kissed him deeply, begging him with her body and tongue to peel off the dress.

He got the hint.

Seconds later, Candis's dress was in a pool of fabric around her feet. She knew he'd missed her without his saying a word. He picked her up, and she wrapped her legs around him as he carried her to the bed. She squeezed her thighs tight. She wanted him to feel the heartbeat in her pussy. She wanted him to understand he was the one who made her "pocketbook" pulsate.

He laid her down on the bed ever so gently and kissed her from top to bottom, making sure to give certain areas extra attention. Candis loved the way he took her dark chocolate, Hershey's Kiss nipples in his mouth and suckled them as if he were a starving newborn. He got her ready, then worked his way down, burying his head between her legs. This was almost—*almost*—her favorite part. He used his tongue to drive her crazy, flicking it over her clit again and again while two fingers massaged her insides, expertly hitting her G-spot. Candis couldn't take it anymore. She wanted him inside her before she came. She scooted away from his mouth and fingers. He came up for air and kissed her. Then Candis, in her eagerness, grabbed his dick and stuffed it inside her. Perfect. Everything about him was perfect. They made love until they fell asleep. She never made it back to the party, and she missed Linda giving big kudos to the new blood and the new direction the company was going.

Linda meant a lot to Candis; she was sort of a surrogate mother and the person with whom she shared many of her feelings about love, life, and work. Candis's mom had died—killed by a drunk driver—when Candis was three and her sister was ten. The whole family was totally devastated. Their mom was their rock. Their dad could barely recover enough to go back to work. For a long time, he couldn't even walk around the house without bursting into sudden bouts of tears. It was too much, and he had to move them out of the house. Ashley, her sister, never forgave their dad for moving and quitting on the memories, but he just couldn't stand the pain of living with the ghost of his wife in every room. She was everywhere—from the dishes, to the wedding photos, to the kids' baby clothes in the closet. He tried to suffer in silence and be strong for the girls, but he reluctantly accepted the insurance settlement and moved them into a new home, leaving most of his wife's things behind. Unbeknownst to the girls until later in life, he never sold the house.

Their mom's friend Jennifer had always liked the girls and helped their dad through his pain. In the beginning, she was a shoulder to lean on. Eventually, hers was the hand he held in marriage. Ashley made life hell for her father and Jennifer, though. She was extremely rebellious and didn't hide the fact that she didn't like their arrangement.

Candis always felt Ashley was a spoiled brat who had everything handed to her on a silver platter. One day, when they were in the mall, a talent scout stopped their stepmom and asked if she would bring Ashley to a photo shoot. She did, and the photographer said Ashley was a natural, that it was one of the best shoots he'd ever done. He sent out the pictures and received hundreds of requests, and just like that, Ashley was a high-demand model in the making. But then, almost as quickly as it started, she threw it away because she didn't like waking up early or sitting in the chairs for hours getting her hair and makeup done. She was about to make loads of money but just stopped going. She later told her dad and Jennifer that she was over it, plain and simple. Her dad was frustrated at her lack of motivation but felt guilty for pushing her too much after her mom died.

Meanwhile, no one even noticed Candis, the dark one in the family. Her stepmom was light skinned, and her dad had fair skin. Candis always resented her sister and despised how life just seemed to fall in her lap. Her sister got pregnant her third year in college—or, as Candis would say, her third freshman year—by this up-and-coming guy who was soaring above the clouds. Very popular, intelligent, handsome, and successful, he started a business in college that was bought by a software company before he graduated. He was already self-made the day he took off his cap and gown. Ashley's life was set; meanwhile, Candis had to work twice as hard just to be noticed.

And now she was in this hotel room with her guy, missing the speech by the one person who had noticed her. She felt bad but couldn't dwell on it, not with her man showing her how much he'd missed her.

Meanwhile, back at the party, Linda stepped off stage, very happy with herself. Her speech had been well received. The crowd laughed when she wanted it to laugh and seemed to be struck by the inspirational quotes she'd laced into the speech. She talked about the passing of the torch to the younger generation and called for more involvement in the community, giving back, and following the dreams of our youth. She encouraged thoughtfulness, honesty in the workplace, and humility. She shared the pain of losing her husband, her first instance of discussing it publicly, pausing at times to regain her composure. The speech was heartfelt and would be talked about for months at the company. And Candis had missed the entire thing because of a guy.

Candis knew Linda would be furious, but it would have to wait until Monday.

Linda ran to the bathroom, high on endorphins, looking for Candis to celebrate her success. "Has anyone seen Candis?" she asked when she found the bathroom empty.

Kevin heard her and mumbled, "I think she ran downstairs for a minute."

Linda grabbed her purse and discovered she had a text from Candis: "Sorry Linda. I had to run out."

She was furious. She knew exactly what had pulled Candis from her speech. "That fucking little bitch!"

Linda

On Monday morning, Linda stormed into the office looking for Candis, still fuming about what went down at the party. She waited in Candis's office, sitting in the red chair she'd helped pick out, and kicked her shoes off. She had on a pair of Louboutins that were really cute but did a number on her feet. She waited for what felt like an hour but was closer to fifteen minutes, getting angrier and angrier at Candis's disrespect, especially after everything she had done for her.

"I mean, I've bent over backwards for this ungrateful little shit!" Linda thought.

She got up and went to the restroom. Her morning coffee was running through her faster than she wanted, and her anger only made matters worse. Her eyes were watering. She looked at herself in the mirror, admiring her outfit but also focusing on the three lines developing on her forehead.

"I'm not growing old gracefully," she thought. She didn't feel old, but her body was changing. All she could think about was her dad saying, "Beauty fades my dear, but competence lasts forever."

She stormed out and headed back toward Candis's office, stopping by her secretary's desk on her way to check messages and grab her phone. She glanced at the screen and noticed a few e-mails. She opened the first. It was from the senior VP of the local Red Cross chapter asking her to attend yet another charity event. She also noticed several missed calls from Justin and wondered what he could possibly want that early in the morning.

Just then, Gina, her new secretary, stood up quickly, almost knocking her coffee out of her hand and startling Linda. "Linda! Your nine o'clock is early, and your son called because he couldn't get you on the line."

Linda looked at Gina with surprise and disappointment. The girl was cute, but her dress was a little shorter than it should be. She thought Gina was good but would probably go out of her way to sleep her way to the top. She didn't have much education—she was barely out of community college—and probably had gotten this far on her looks. She was biracial, but she could pass for white if she dyed her hair blond. She had big hips, a small waist, and a flat stomach. She had medium-sized boobs, but she kept them pushed up to make them look larger. The seniors at the company loved to stop by Linda's office to catch a glimpse of Gina.

Kevin had been in charge of bringing Gina on, and the first time Linda set eyes on her, she said, "Kevin, did you hire Barbie to be my goddamn secretary?"

Linda went back to the other end of the building and down four flights of stairs to get to Candis's office. She needed to walk off her anger, but it wasn't working. She was fuming.

She picked up the phone to call her son.

"What's up, Ma?" Justin asked.

"You called me, buddy. You tell me what's up," Linda hit back.

"Oh...I was just gonna ask if I could head out to the beach house this weekend. Unless you were using it?" His voice was sheepish.

"Of course, baby. Do you have money?"

"Yeah. I'm good, Ma."

"Okay, baby." She was filled with happiness at the thought of Justin and how much she loved him. Then she thought of Candis, and her anger resurged.

Candis walked into the building with a smile so bright it lit up the day. She was singing, content with her situation in life. She'd had a great weekend with her man, and they were planning to take a long trip to an undisclosed location. She loved surprises and could barely contain herself. She couldn't wait until her life was perfect. She said good morning to everyone she passed in the hall. She was on a high as she ran to the elevator.

Just then, her phone rang, It was her sister. Candis answered with a smile. "Hey girl. How was your weekend? Her voice was filled with excitement, anticipating her sister's asking about her weekend in response. Candis was funny like that, often fishing for compliments and validation.

"Campbell was out of town on business again this weekend," Ashley snapped. "I mean…if he keeps this up, we may not see him for the rest of the year."

Candis tried to calm her sister. She changed the subject, feeling guilty for the awesome weekend she'd had with her man. "How's Cooper holding up?"

Cooper was Candis's six-year-old nephew, whom she absolutely adored. He was the one thing that kept her visiting her sister's house when Campbell was away. Her sister often called to talk whenever her husband was out of town. Candis felt like Ashley didn't listen and only called to vent. Ashley was always venting. Still, Candis was content with their relationship. Her sister was the only real family she had, and she wanted to make it work. Once she had remarked to a friend, "If we weren't sisters, we wouldn't be friends."

"How's Cooper doing at the new school?" she asked, keeping her voice light. There was silence.

"Did you hear me?"

"You're breaking up," Ashley said impatiently. "It's probably because you're on that elevator. Okay, I got you now. Well, girl…he's not being bullied anymore, but I'm not really sure if he likes the new teachers. It's always different because he doesn't have the older or younger sibling like we had growing up."

Candis exited the elevator and headed toward her office, but she immediately noticed something out of place. The door was open, and she was sure she had closed it when she left the day before. Her OCD kicked in. "Ash, I gotta call you back," she said quickly. "Bye!"

She walked into her office and was startled to find Linda there. "Linda!" she exclaimed. There was just a hint of guilt in her voice.

"You were too busy fucking to come send your buddy off?" Linda said, her tone throwing Candis so much that she almost dropped her things. "Where were you on the one day I asked you to be there for me?"

Linda was visibly shaken and fought to hold back tears. "Can you not suck a dick for a few minutes while I retire and give you all kind of motherfuckin' shout-outs? Honestly, girl. You need to get your life together and get your priorities straight. There's more to life than a goddamn dick!"

Candis's eyes were wide. She had just been soaring high on life, and now she was standing in her doorway with Linda lighting into her.

"What hold does this man have over you? And why are you so damn careless around him?"

Linda's eyes flashed. She had warned Candis about dating older men—men just like the one she was dating. As much as Candis respected her, she thought Linda's relationship advice was unreasonable and outdated.

Linda was out the game, wed to a fairytale husband scenario that didn't exist now and probably never had.

"Linda," she said slowly. "It's not fair to judge someone you don't even know. We're in love." She couldn't help but smile when she said the last part.

"Wipe that goddamn smile off your face! Honey, I don't need to meet him to know him. I've had my share of men, and the one you're dealing with is a no good piece of shit! Sorry to tell you. Oh, and he'll never commit. What worries me is that you can't see it. You're still in dreamland."

"Linda, I'm so sorry."

"Keep your goddamn sorry. Every time I turn around since you met this guy, it's always 'I'm sorry' or 'Forgive me' or 'Can you cover for me.'"

Linda could be a terror in the boardroom, but Candis had never heard this much fury in her voice. She was clearly sad, but she was bordering on manic, too—like she was desperate to get through to her young protégée. But Candis couldn't focus. Her mind floated back to the previous night and then to the next time she'd be with her man. She thought about his body on her body, their back and forth. She couldn't wait to see him again.

"Do you even hear me?" Linda snapped. She stormed out of Candis's office, more upset than she'd been since before her husband died. Candis couldn't help it—Linda reminded her of every mistake she'd made through the years. She went to her office and cried at the thought of Candis's inevitable broken heart. Candis was in love, though, and no matter what anyone said, she wouldn't see anything until it was too late.

Candis, the dreamer, always responded to Linda's concerns with something along the lines of: "I'll be fine. I'm enjoying myself, and besides, how many times will I be young?"

Linda worried about Candis's carefree attitude but understood that women often have to find themselves before they stop chasing men.

Linda hated the fact that Candis was potentially destroying her career and wasting her beauty on somebody twelve years her senior. And the guy was *married*. He had a *family*. Candis was too smart to deal with that shit. The whole thing was a recipe for disaster. "Why not date someone her own age?" she thought. "What will she learn from this guy that she can't learn from someone her own age? And why date a man who was already committed elsewhere?" Linda had gone through similar experiences several times in her youth; she'd heard all the "I love yous," "I'll leave hers," "Just wait for mes," et cetera. She'd heard it *all*, and as much as she didn't want to harp on the matter, she couldn't sit back and watch it happen to Candis without trying to do something. She knew where things were heading. She had moved to different cities for these men, planned her life around them, and waited for marriage proposals that never came. She had been disappointed every single time. The last time it happened—before she met her late husband, Jim—she took an entire bottle of Advil and woke up in the ER. She simply couldn't, in good conscience, be passive and wait around for that predictable shit to happen to her dear friend.

The previous year, when Linda and Candis met, she'd seen something very familiar in the young woman. Linda couldn't quite put her finger on it but liked it nonetheless. Candis was confident and attractive, and she ranked much better than the other dingbats Linda had interviewed. Of course, her instinct was on the money. Candis had an excellent work ethic, a way with people, and reminded Linda of a younger version of herself. Early on, Linda made it her mission to ensure that Candis succeeded, and once Linda took an interest in someone, she was set. Linda was worshipped at the company, and the fact that she took on a young protégée caught everyone's attention. Soon, Candis, the junior consultant, was getting added visibility on all of her projects. Candis enjoyed the attention and being good at her job. It didn't take long before she could envision herself rising the corporate ladder—all the way to the top of the company.

After Linda left, Candis, still stunned from the berating she'd just received, sat at her desk and tried to work.

"Hey, you okay?" A voice came from the doorway, and she looked up to see Kevin standing half in and half out of her office.

Candis just shook her head, her joyful glow replaced by sadness. She had gone from floating on clouds to having the worst day—all before her morning coffee was finished.

"You want to grab lunch later or you want to talk about it?"

She didn't answer. She really didn't have time for Kevin and sort of waved him off. Her mentor had just let her have it, and she was feeling sorry for herself. She closed her door and cried for twenty minutes, ignoring her ringing office and cell phones.

Finally, her secretary opened the door. "Hey Candis. I rescheduled your morning so you'll be fine if you need to take an early lunch or leave."

"Thanks, Bea," Candis said softly. She thought about just going home. How could she continue the rest of the day after what Linda had just said? She picked up her phone and saw a text from Campbell: "Call me when you have a minute." She was too somber for that. She put down the phone and went to the bathroom two floors down so she wouldn't have to run into anyone from her floor. Gossip spread so fast in the office, and she didn't want to hear all of the "Girl, I'm so sorry about what happeneds." She started to think that she might need to look for work elsewhere. It all sort of hit her at once while she was walking out of the bathroom. There was a lot of uncertainty, and to make matters worse, she hadn't had her period. "Please, Lord," she thought. "Don't let me be pregnant again."

Almost two weeks passed, and Candis didn't hear anything from Linda. She figured their relationship was over, and more and more, it felt like her job was, too. But she held out some hope that Linda was just busy. Linda had been working out of the country and would not return for another day or so.

While Linda was in Lima, Peru, strengthening the company's international ties, she thought a lot about what she had said to Candis and really wanted to make amends. It wasn't the girl's fault. She was still learning and growing. Linda had just let the pain from her past bubble up and get the best of her.

"I should call her," she said out loud. Then she picked up the phone and dialed.

Candis was sitting at home watching TV. She picked up on the first ring, thinking it was her man.

"Hey, girl."

Candis started to cry almost immediately. She hadn't realized quite how badly she'd wanted to hear from Linda. She grabbed the remote and put the TV on mute. There was a long pause, and then she said, "Linda, I'm so so sorry. I never meant to hurt you. I don't really know what's gotten into me. I truly appreciate everything you've done for me, and I don't want it to come off as unappreciative."

Linda shed a few tears and grabbed the hotel puffs by the desk to wipe her face. "Look, sweetie. I really want to apologize for letting you have it. You didn't deserve it like that—and so publicly. My temper got the best of me, and my love for you got the rest. You're a great young woman, and we all write our own stories, mistakes, experiences, or whatever you want to call them."

Candis stopped crying long enough to say, "I'm just glad you called me. I'm a mess, and I just need to get my life together."

Linda responded in a very caring tone. "Is everything okay? Are you guys still seeing each other?"

Candis cleared her throat and said, "Well, I haven't had my period yet." Then she started to cry again. "Please don't say I told you so. I can't take any more of that."

"Aww, baby. I'm so sorry for making you feel that way and saying those things. You're my girl, and you always have been. Everything will be okay. We'll figure it out like we always do. Get back to bed."

"Thanks Linda. Love you."

"Love you, too, baby."

Linda hung up the phone and lay down to watch TV, but she couldn't stop thinking about young Candis. "What will we do about her?" she wondered. She shook her head as another tear rolled down her cheek.

Lance and Sydney

ance was leaving work when he remembered BP had a
dollar deal for a hotdog and a drink on Wednesdays. He
loved hump day; he didn't have to think about dinner, and
he loved hotdogs. He had since he was a kid. They were the
first things he could make for himself. Lance was a handsome
young man, built like a long-distance runner or basketball
player—tall, light complexioned, with long muscles. His body
was still somewhat chiseled from his training days, despite
going through a rough patch and a severe fall from grace.
It was a long drop from being the star sprinter of the track
team—an Olympic hopeful and the fastest guy in Lexington,
Virginia—to what he was now: a janitor.

Both his parents ran track and field, and he was a natural
for the sport. Things began to go south when his sister died,
though. He was really close to his older sister (they were
separated by only two years) and thought the world of
her. She died as a result of an accident his senior year in

college. A few hours before the accident, they were hanging out with friends from their childhood, laughing and joking together on a break from school for the holidays. But when the drinks started coming out, his sister bailed. She wasn't having it. She'd been opposed to drinking ever since a drunk driver sideswiped her car. "I'm out," she said to Lance, and as she said it, she took off running with a smile. He barely had time to react. He jumped up and started chasing her. It was about six blocks to their house from their friend's home. They were always competitive, and it always got the best of them. They couldn't resist a race.

They split up. His sister was faster but not as athletic. She took a dirt trail behind the neighborhood store. The Rottweiler from the junkyard got loose and started to chase her, bringing back memories from their childhood. The dog was not as fast as he used to be, but he still gave a good chase. She outsmarted him, switching her path several times. No one knew the woods better than she did. It had become sort of a game to them growing up in the woods—the dog always chased them. She took it for granted that there were never any vehicles on the path, even though it was wide enough for a car or an occasional dirt bike.

She was almost home when it happened. She looked up and saw the house, then caught a glimpse of Lance from the corner of her eye. "Suck it loser!" she yelled and laughed as she ran up the trail to where it opened to an intersection.

"Watch out Rachel!" he screamed.

She didn't hear him over her headphones. He was always on her case about listening to music too loud.

She didn't see the truck as she sprinted into the intersection, and it hit her, knocking her almost twenty feet in the air. Lance ran over and attempted to resuscitate her, but she went into a coma immediately and was pronounced brain dead only days later.

Lance was inconsolable. He blamed himself for not being able to save her, even though the doctors said she had an aneurysm and there was nothing they could do. She was on life support, but Lance's parents didn't want her to suffer. They pulled the plug after three weeks. Lance felt it was downright murder. He started drinking the next day, and when that didn't work any longer, he moved on to more potent ways to suppress his feelings. He couldn't forgive them for killing his sister. He felt like they never gave him an opportunity to right his wrong.

He decided to move far away from home. The memories were just too much to bear. He completely cut contact with his parents and his friends. He cut all ties to his former life—anything that reminded him of Rachel—and worked a series of odd jobs around the country before settling in Cadensville, California.

All of that led to the life he was living now and the Wednesday deal at BP. About five years after high school, with few job prospects in sight, everyone wondered what had happened to the promising child of the former track stars. He was a sad mess, but he wanted to get his life back together and work through his issues.

As he was leaving the gas station, he noticed this young, attractive woman signaling for his attention. He initially assumed she'd mistaken him for someone else or was gesturing to someone behind him. He hoped it was him, though. She was striking—no makeup but a natural beauty. She walked with a confidence that was familiar, but he couldn't place her. He turned around but soon realized she was pointing at him and waving him over.

"Hey, please watch Junior. I gotta pee."

He looked at her, and she gave him a hand gesture as if to say, "The kid in the blue Honda Accord with the worn tires." Lance poked his head in the car, and there was Junior in his car seat. He was wearing a bib covered in some old spit-up, but he was adorable: a friendly little guy with hazel eyes and hair mussed all over his round head. He offered a wide smile as soon as Lance looked in at him.

Lance took inventory of the car and determined it could use a good cleaning. There were food wrappers and receipts all over the floor. "There's no way this girl has a guy," he thought. "Who would let their girl ride around like this?" He looked up and saw that the gas tank was on empty. He jumped out and started pumping gas, talking to Junior the whole time. "It's gonna be okay, lil' guy. I just need to pump some gas so you and your mom can get out of here." He was that type of guy, always doing nice things for people and going out of his way to help.

With Junior smiling and cooing in the backseat, Lance couldn't help but think about his own mortality. It's funny how life's small triggers can give your system the jolt it needs at just the right time.

The woman was gone for only a few minutes, but it seemed like an hour to Lance as he reflected on the steps that had led him to that gas station at that moment. Junior was about a year old, charming, and had the nicest eyes and caramel skin. "You're gonna be a lady killer, lil' guy," Lance said to him. "Those eyes alone will get you in the door."

As Junior made a gurgling noise and connected with Lance, it hit him. "That's it," he thought. "I want a kid. I've got to get my life back on track."

He looked up as Junior's mom walked out of the store. Something about the way she moved was so familiar. He couldn't quite pinpoint it, but she reminded him of Tera, a girl he dated in college before the accident.

"Thank you so much," she said. "I promise I'm not a horrible mother, and thanks for not kidnapping my kid. We've been driving from my mom's place, and I really had to go and didn't want to take the car seat and get him all riled up."

"No problem," Lance said with a smile. "This little guy was a joy. I was glad to help."

He was getting up to leave when she said, "Please let me return the favor. Take this twenty."

He shook his head. "I couldn't. I was happy to do it. It made me feel whole."

"Well, I'll cook your favorite meal," she insisted.

"That won't be necessary, ma'am. Trust me when I tell you, I got more out of the experience than old Junior there."

"Do you have any kids?" she asked.

"No, but your little guy kinda makes me wish I did have a few of my own."

"Please let me cook for you," she said, handing him her phone for him to type in his number. He took it, punching it in, then handed it back.

"Good. Now I'll have you in my phone for when I cook. And you better answer, Mr.—?"

"LJ," he said.

"Okay, LJ. Kinda like LL Cool J?"

"Sure, whatever," he said with a half frown.

"Thanks again!"

She called that night, and he went over. They were linked from that point forward. It only took about a week for them to move in together. They quickly settled into a routine of playing house like they'd known each other forever.

It felt right, but Lance couldn't help wonder if they were moving too fast.

Sydney smiled and said, "Hey, when I get tired of you, I'll let you know." They both let it go.

Lance was at home one day when a life insurance commercial came on as they were watching the game.

"Syd?" he said.

"Yeah, babe?"

"How do you go to the doctor? What about Junior?"

"We go to the clinic or the emergency room if we absolutely have to go." She shot him a questioning look.

He was debating whether he could get them on the health insurance plan through his janitorial job. They had an arrangement: he paid the utility bills, and she would go to Vegas frequently to help care for her grandmother. She always returned with some cash. Her mom was her grandmother's lone caretaker, so it really helped when Sydney could lend a hand. Sydney was always looking for unique ways to make quick cash because it was hard for her to keep a steady job. She really liked Lance. He was an all-American guy and really knew how to do things around the house. He could cook, bake, clean, grocery shop, and fix anything. It was as if she had found some girl's long-lost husband and moved in with him.

But she had a burning secret she was dying to tell him. She just kept finding reasons to put it off. "What if he rejects me?" she thought. "He's so good with Junior. He's so good to me and just an all-around great guy."

That night when they went to bed, she was hoping she'd finally find the courage to tell him. The more she delayed it, the more the memories haunted her.

Sydney had struggled when she first got into the life. She never wanted to dance at the club or do anything else that line of work required, but she was fine being a waitress. It wasn't until her boyfriend came up short on rent—again—that she was propelled into the life she lived now. She and her boyfriend were about to get evicted from their apartment. Her friend Dixie (later Dave) overheard her and gave her an opportunity that required her to sleep with one of the clients at the club. She was hesitant at first, but she really needed the money. It hurt to think about the fact that someone other than her man would be inside of her. She had never cheated on any of her boyfriends. She was not wired that way and was always referred to as a "good girl." The only time she had issues was in her youth, when one of her cousins got a bit too aggressive with her and tried to take advantage of her beauty and her body.

When she and Dixie arrived at the guy's room, she almost walked out.

"D, I'm not sure I can go through with this, but I really need this money."

"Girl, you better get yo' shit together and git this money!" Dixie said. "We don't play 'bout shit like this, and you need this cash. Hell…I need this money, too. Don't think about it, baby. Just do it."

Sydney went in the room, undressed, and closed her eyes, taking her mind somewhere else. Later, she would describe it to her friends as entering a new phase in her life—"almost like crossing over in a biblical sense." She developed a few regular clients, eventually branching out and securing a stable client base of her own. She had many offers from guys who wanted to marry her, but she always worried about her son. Lance was the first guy she ever let around Junior, and it seemed to be working out fine. Still, she was extremely hesitant about telling him about her past.

Of course, Lance had his own pain and secrets that he was reluctant to talk about. Sydney didn't know a lot about him and the loss he was dealing with.

Before he met Sydney, Lance had been a functioning alcoholic who worked only to support himself and to stay away from the memories of his sister. She was everywhere he looked: in the parlor, in the pub, in the grocery store. The food he liked to eat and even the clothes he wore conjured up her teasing voice: "You're still a dork."

Lance stopped drinking cold turkey when he moved in with Sydney. He didn't want to drink around the baby. His dad had dropped his sister while drunk when they were kids, and he never forgot how his mom reacted to it. She almost killed him. No, he would never drink around a kid. But he didn't just stop drinking. He started working out again and started reading to expand his mind. He wanted to be better for her, and suddenly, maxims he'd heard but ignored over the years started trickling into his mind: "The best lesson is a bought lesson." "Bloom where you're planted." "Do unto others." He was hearing them in stereo and heeding the advice, but at the same time, he sensed Sydney was nervous about taking their relationship further.

She was worried he wouldn't accept her past, and he was worried she wouldn't accept his. They were both kind people at heart, and they always found a way to compromise. He saw his sister in Sydney and wanted to help her more and more. She saw an ex boyfriend, Lamar, in Lance and wanted to help him, too. Lamar was the captain of the football team at Johnson State University. He was extremely popular. Everyone wanted him, and Sydney had fallen instantly in love with him. She loved Lamar more than anything in the world, and Lance brought back a lot of those dormant feelings.

"Hey, babe. Are you free this weekend to watch Junior?"

"Yeah, what's up?" Lance asked. "It's your grandma again, isn't it?"

She just looked at him, and her eyes filled with sadness. Her grandmother, who had stage IV ovarian cancer, was the only person who never judged her for being who she was. She could tell her grandmother about her many adventures, and the old woman would give her advice about the men she was seeing. Sydney had a lot of irons in the fire, and she was juggling multiple balls at any given time: her profession, her relationships, and motherhood. She made it look easy, but in reality, she was struggling. She didn't want to lie to Lance, but she really liked having him around and couldn't bear the thought of him judging her. She was honest about her grandmother but not so much about anything else. She gave him a big hug and said thank you. Her bags were packed, and she was headed to Vegas in the morning.

Lance and Junior had plans to go to the park. It made Lance feel responsible and like an adult. Without realizing it, Sydney was helping Lance grow into his own.

As he was getting ready to go out, Lance went to the baby's room to get a diaper bag and spotted a peculiar number of bags under Junior's bed. He knelt down to retrieve one. When he pulled it out, he found it was stuffed with $20 and $100 bills. There must have been $20,000 in there. He pulled out another bag, and it was filled with just as much money. Then he stopped going through the bags. He didn't know the circumstances and didn't want to judge.

"Maybe there's a legitimate explanation for this," he thought.

Bianca

Sydney was hanging out with Dave at one of his favorite restaurants when he introduced her to his cousin Bianca. She was a young woman, somewhere between twenty-four and twenty-seven, and Sydney presumed she was in the same business and only in town for a couple days on some odd jobs and special requests. She was beautiful; she looked to be of Native American descent, and her energy seemed to elevate the mood in the room. She walked like a model on the runway, and when she spoke, it sounded like she was from the upper Northwest but with a highly educated tone. She talked like one of Sydney's professors from school.

Sydney would find out later that Bianca was, in fact, a dropout from the Medical School at the University of Washington, bored with a life of trying to impress her parents, friends, and teachers. She and a friend had flown out to Vegas on a whim after finals. She was hanging out in the bar at Trump Towers when she met a group of guys.

One of the guys—a big dude with the broad shoulders of a football player—invited them over, and she sat with him and his friends all day. They discussed football, life, drinking; they were flirting pretty heavily.

"Your eyes are beautiful," she told him. "There's so much wisdom in them. You look like you've seen and heard a lot."

He smiled and kept pouring her drinks. He knew exactly what he was doing and needed her to be drunk. "Drink up, baby. It's all on us, don't you worry."

He was making her feel more and more comfortable with every drink. She was having a wonderful time and not really worried about anything. The guy invited her back to his room, to the dismay of her friend. "We don't even know these guys," her friend said. "Let's go!" She started to walk off, gesturing for Bianca to follow, but Bianca wanted to continue her good time.

"I'll see you back at the room," she told her friend, who walked away angrily.

"Let's go, baby. Where's your room?" Bianca asked.

The guy smiled and led her off. Then they started having a really good time. Alcohol flowed and music blared. He was smoking, too, but Bianca had never smoked anything in her life and decided not to try tonight. Her mother was a drug addict, and she didn't want to ever have those types of problems.

They danced to all the old rap hits, including Juvenile's "Drop It Like It's Hot" and Mystikal's "Shake Ya Ass." Bianca was bringing out all her best moves, and after one song finished, they both collapsed on the bed. He was sitting close enough for her to smell the liquor wafting on his breath.

He leaned in for a kiss, and Bianca was ready for it. She'd been wanting to kiss him all night. They began having a full-blown make-out session, kissing and caressing each other. Bianca was enjoying it. She thought about something her best friend always said: "A little kissing never hurt anyone." This guy's kisses were amazing. She had never been kissed like that before; it felt like the way she always should have been kissed. She was turned on but wasn't ready to go all the way with him. She'd just had a bad break-up with a low-life boyfriend and didn't want to rush back into anything on the rebound.

The guy had already told his friends he was gonna smash, but it was apparent as he kept trying to move her shirt off her shoulder and she kept putting it back on that they weren't on the same page. "We're just kissing," she told herself. "I mean, I really want him, but I'm no ho." Besides, what did she know about him? She could sense he had other plans. He kept kissing and rubbing her thigh. Before she knew it, his hand was up her skirt, reaching for her Vickies. She wanted her secret to stay a secret, so she grabbed his hand and pulled her skirt back down. It was too late. She tried to stop him, but there was nothing she could do. He was so strong.

"Please," she begged. "You don't have to do this. Stop."

She began to cry as he pulled her clothes off. She struggled, but it didn't even slow him down. He pushed her onto the bed with her ass up and stomach pressed into the mattress. Bianca yelled for help, but no one could hear her muffled cries. He forced his way on her and inside her. Bianca had never felt a pain so raw and vile. How had this happened to her? He pumped himself roughly in and out of her for five minutes and came inside of her. Then he pulled his pants up, finished the rest of his drink, and left her in the hotel room.

She was paralyzed. She didn't call the police. She was drunk, he was high, and she knew no one would believe her. She never should have come to the room in the first place, and now here she was. Who would believe she didn't want it? Look at what she was wearing. It was obviously her fault for allowing this to happen. She had horrible thoughts about what would happen next. She had visions of walking into oncoming traffic or harming herself. She was pissed and wanted to get back at this guy. She would kill him, she thought, if she ever had the opportunity.

She couldn't move for days after the attack. She stayed in her room, ordering room service. Her friend didn't really understand what was happening to her and ended up leaving her in Vegas. She blamed herself for months after the attack and could not bring herself to tell anyone about it but Dave.

Dave had heard about these guys doing numbers on girls at the hotel. There wasn't much Dave didn't hear about. He was the chief concierge, always in the know. All the talk passed through him. It was his hidden passion and also a way for him to hide in plain sight. Folks didn't even know he was the person they were afraid of because he looked like a nice, clean-cut, suit-wearing concierge.

Bianca walked into the bar, and Dave turned around, smiled, and greeted her.

She started crying as soon as she locked eyes with him. She told him everything that had happened.

"Oh, we gonna get that motherfucker, don't you worry."

She couldn't stop crying. Dave took her up to his room and had a doctor come by to check on her. He did some digging to find out who this guy was who would dare to harm his family. Dave loved his family, but most of them were not accepting of his alternative life choices. He especially favored Bianca. She was always kind to him and reminded him of a younger version of himself. He hadn't seen her in almost seven years, since the last family reunion. They always let religion get in the way. Dave was the only "queer" in the family, and his lifestyle didn't fit with their beliefs.

Bianca had come to visit Dave to experience city life. She had never been to Vegas before, and she wanted a break from life at home and to see what all the hype was about. "I'm not going back to that life," Bianca told him. "I'm tired of living the life that everyone wants me to live. I have things I want to do, and I'm also tired of always being the good girl. I came out here to have a good time, but I didn't know he was gonna do this to me."

She really opened up to Dave. The same thing had happened to him when he was younger, at the hands of one of his now-deceased uncles. Dave took care of that problem and then left the area. Everyone knew his uncle was molesting him, but they kept looking the other way because the man was a pastor. When he drowned, most people thought it was an accident—except those who knew what was going on.

Bianca wanted to get out of Vegas that night, but Dave implored her to stay. Sydney thought Bianca was the most beautiful woman she had ever seen in her life, and it immediately woke up some latent feelings of bisexuality in her. She wanted to be with Bianca and gave her a look that said, "Later, but it will happen." She had been talking business with Dave before the girl walked into the bar but then had to run up to her room to turn a trick.

"Can we meet at the spot in the morning?" Sydney asked Dave as she gathered her purse.

"Yes, see you there."

The next morning, he brought Bianca with him to meet Sydney at the little hole-in-the wall restaurant where they always met. Dave really wanted to know how Bianca was doing mentally because he remembered how hard it had been for him.

"I can't believe I let this happen to me. I'm so stupid," she said, shaking her head.

"Aw suga', this ain't your fault. Trust me. It happens to everyone in some shape or form. I'm just happy that you have your health." Dave said, patting her back. "I had something similar happen to me when I was young, and it was at the hands of a family member."

Dave started to get emotional. Bianca could see his eyes starting to water. It seemed as if he were about to lose it, and then his phone rang.

"What's up man?" he said, pulling himself together. "Uh huh, okay. Okay. Yeah…we'll take it from here."

He looked at Bianca and handed her a gun. Then he explained the phone call: "Today may be your day for justice."

Just then, Sydney walked in and waved to them.

"Be cool," Dave said softly to Bianca. "I know where he's gonna be later, and he might just get an opportunity to apologize to you in person."

Candis

Candis was fantasizing about her man and the trip they had just taken. He was really something else—always full of surprises. But then her mind drifted back to reality. Here she was, headed out of town alone. Alone again on a weekend when she really needed him. She was on a journey she never wanted to be on and was filled with anxiety over what was about to happen.

It was a three-and-a-half-hour drive—plenty of time to call him, but once again he was unavailable. Maybe he was playing with his kid, at soccer practice, or just doing family stuff. She was lost in her thoughts: "I'm so tired of this shit. Every time I need him, he's not around. He always complains about being so unhappy with her, but every time I need him, he's not available. If he's so happy with me, then why can't he commit? Why can't he marry me, have kids, the whole nine yards? Why am I pregnant and on my way to an abortion clinic? How did this happen? Why can't we have it? Why can't I be the one? I'm such an idiot!"

She wanted to cry. She was in love with a man who truly didn't love her back. If he did love her, he would pick up the phone, she thought. "If he did love me, he would be here with me right now." She wanted to hate him, but she couldn't forget his kindness, his warmth, and how much he said he loved her. She kept telling herself that over and over. He really loved her and only her. They would be together someday. Every song that played on the radio reminded her of the many jet-setting adventures they'd had over the last few months.

Her thoughts were interrupted when her phone rang.

"Hey girl, what are you doing?"

It was her friend Gayle. "Driving."

"You're really going?"

"Yep, I'm making it up this highway now."

"He's not with you, is he?" Gayle said in a very "I told you so" tone. The line went quiet.

"Candis? Hey...are you okay?"

"I gotta go," Candis said quickly. "I'll talk to you later."

Her eyes swelled with tears again. She felt so foolish and alone. She'd been lying to her stepmom for weeks about her so-called illness and making excuses for not coming around. She wasn't really showing, but she didn't want to take the chance that someone would guess. She was so successful in her professional life, fresh out of business school and already working as a consultant. It might have started with the influential pull of her dad, but her grades, quick wit, and candor had kept her in the door. She was crushing it professionally. But her personal life was a mess.

As she arrived at the clinic in New Haven, she gathered her thoughts and stepped out of the car. It seemed like five miles to the door from the parking lot, and there was a sea of protestors. "Fucking great," she thought. "As if I didn't feel bad enough. These motherfuckers want to protest today?"

They chanted and pointed their venomous signs at her. "Murderer!" one sign read. "You are killing!" screamed another sign, and yet another blared, "Go to hell you sorry whore!" One lady attempted to reach out to her, saying, "You don't have to do it, honey. Let me help you."

"Sorry lady, but you can't help me," she said as she pushed past.

Her nerves were frayed. She couldn't stop shaking as she walked into the clinic. Then she saw couples working through their pain together and got pissed all over again. She sat there, questioning the decision until the nurse called, "Sheila Jackson." No one answered, and then it hit her: that was the fake name she'd given to keep her real name out of the records. She was paying for the termination with cash so nothing could be traced back to her.

The nurse took her vitals and asked her to change into a blue gown. She was gentle and sweet, as if she'd done this a million times before. "Lie on the table, please," she said, patting it. Candis climbed up. It was cold and smelled like death—the death of a thousand children. "Open up and relax," the nurse said. "I've got it from here." The table was so awful it was almost enough in itself to make Candis get out of there.

Then it happened. In hindsight, the nurse must have been pro-life because she didn't pull the curtain back. Was she intentionally trying to get Candis to watch as the fetus moved around during the ultrasound? Did she want Candis to have second thoughts? Her mind drifted to baby names: Jacob, Matthew, Brent. Would he look more like his dad or her? She thought about him playing football, being good at math, getting a full ride to Baylor, or USC, or Stanford. She was filled with excitement and bright ideas for a future that would never come. She was eighteen weeks pregnant. She almost got up from the table twice.

She propped herself on her elbows. "I can't—" she started to say, but then she thought about the gravity of the situation and became very, very sad.

"This may feel weird for a minute," the nurse said, "but then you'll be fine. You're going to feel a small stick."

Before Candis realized what was happening, the baby stopped moving. She immediately started crying uncontrollably. The weight of the situation hit her, and she was filled with thoughts of many horrible past decisions. The lies filled her brain, and all she could do was try to collect herself. She thought about the trips she took. Was she fooling herself? "How could I be so stupid!" she said out loud. Then she let go of all the emotions she was trying to keep hidden. There were no cute, watery eyes and tiny gasps. This was the moaning and wailing you saw only at painful funerals.

The nurse tried to calm her down, and other members of the staff rushed in with water, cool towels, and just about anything they felt she might need. She was ready for the procedure to be over. But then the nurse explained that since she was so far along, she would have to return the next day and deliver the dead fetus. Then they could finish up the procedure. She almost fainted. This procedure was brutal enough, but now she had to take the fetus home and come back? It was almost too much for her mind to grasp.

The doctor, an older woman, asked, "Honey, where is the father? Is he aware of what you did today?"

In that moment, Candis felt embarrassment begin to wash over her.

She was so emotional, she could barely speak. "Yeah... but...sorry...but I can't stop crying. He's at home with his...with his...wife...my...my...oh, dear god...my fucking sister! I'm a horrible person! I got pregnant by my sister's husband!"

The head nurse grabbed her and hugged her. Candis was in physical and emotional agony. She was inconsolable. How could she be so awful? It all hit her again like alcohol on an open cut. How could she face her family? She was in love with a man she couldn't have, and there was nothing she could do about it. He was at home with his family, and she was killing any hope they had of their own. How could she be so trapped? The one person she wanted to tell was also the one person she had done the unthinkable to for so long. Was she a horrible person? Why didn't he just leave?

She called him, but he didn't answer. She texted him, but he didn't answer. She called her stepmom, but she didn't answer, either. She called Linda, who also didn't answer. A deep sadness overwhelmed her.

She was suffering, and he didn't even seem to give a shit. How could he not call? "I thought he loved me," she said to herself. "Oh well. Fuck him. For now, at least."

Later that night, he finally called her back. "Hey, you okay, baby?"

His nerve! "Hell no, I'm not okay!" she wanted to say. "I just had to kill another one of our babies. When do I get to keep one? When are you going to leave her?" But she didn't say any of these things. She couldn't talk to him like that. He would set her straight, and that could be the end of them. She didn't want to lose him. Even with their crazy situation, she couldn't see herself without him. Candis would wait as long as she needed to have him to herself. She rolled her eyes at the thought of him playing house all day while she was protecting the life he wanted to maintain, keeping her in the closet. She didn't like him for the first time in their relationship, and the feeling would only build from that point forward.

Candis knew she was playing with fire. How could she be in love with her sister's husband? Although her sister was an evil, stuck-up, entitled bitch, she still didn't deserve to have her whole world come tumbling down at the hands of her own sister.

Campbell

A few weeks had passed since the last time Candis saw Ashley. The last time they spoke, it ended on a bad note with a petty argument. Candis was upset when her sister told her she had gone to the Malibu Bar. That was Candis and Campbell's favorite spot. "He took that bitch?" Candis thought. She was angry with her sister for trying to take her man, even though that was a fucked-up way to look at it. Technically, Cambell was Ashley's man. Candis resented her sister every day for having the perfect life just fall into her lap.

Candis was on her way out of the house to grab a few things from the store, but she couldn't get her garage door to open. She knew just the solution. She would call her sister and get Mr. Fix-It right on it. He could fix the door and give her a fix at the same time.

"Hey girl, what's up?"

"Make it quick, Candis." Ashley snapped. "I'm fixing Cooper's breakfast."

"Girl, my garage is so crazy, it keeps—"

"Getting stuck," Ashley cut her off. "Girl, mine too. Campbell just fixed it. You want me to send him over to look at yours?"

"I mean…if you think he can fix it?" Candis smirked.

"I'll send him over there so I can get a break from his ass. He's been up cleaning everything all morning; he barely sits down when he's home. Please take his ass and find whatever else you can get him to do."

"Oh, I have something for him to do," thought Candis.

"I'll send him right over," Ashley finished.

Campbell got the message from Ashley to get over to Candis's house. He lit up but was also nervous. He hadn't seen her since the abortion a few weeks earlier. He didn't know if she was gonna shoot him with the gun he'd given her or give him passionate sex. He had seen a different side of her the last time they talked—she was clearly upset.

When he pulled up to the house, the garage door was open, and Candis was waiting for him. He walked up, and she said, "I've gotta run." But not before giving him a long, passionate kiss and rubbing her hands over the bulge in his pants. "There it is!" she said with a grin. "I've missed him. Are you gonna be here when I get back?"

He looked her up and down, threw her against the wall, pulled up her skirt, and reached down inside, already knowing she didn't have panties on. Before

Candis could resist, he grabbed the condom out of his pocket and showed her how much he missed her. It had been over two months since they'd had sex, and each of them was longing for the other.

"I want you to cum on my dick," he growled. She had to leave, but she was so close to climaxing and wasn't leaving until she did.

"Please god! Oh my goodness! Get it baby!" she yelled, and they both climaxed together. That's how it normally worked when they were together. Then they both cleaned up and got dressed.

"I made you some sandwiches and put them in the fridge. And please drink some water. I can't have my baby out there sweating too much." Candis gave him a kiss on her way out the door.

"Okay, love. I've got it. We'll have it back to new in no time." He was so handy, she thought, again comparing him to the "boys" she had dealt with up to that point.

He was almost done with the garage when he went inside to use the restroom. He always liked using her bathroom—it was so girly and clean. But on his way through her bedroom, he noticed something under the bed.

"No way," he thought. He knelt, and indeed, there it was: Candis's diary. He paused for a second with the diary in his hands. Should he read it? Or should he respect her privacy and space? It didn't take long to decide. He opened it and started to scan:

> *Today I started sleeping with my sister's husband,*
> *and I have decided that I love him and I want him*
> *to leave her for good.*

"That's pretty bold to put on the first page," he thought.
He read further:

> *Today I called my man, and he was once again*
> *unavailable. I hate that he is with that bitch and*
> *that it makes me feel like shit. Am I not worthy of*
> *his time? His attention? His affection? He doesn't*
> *even know about the first abortion. It belonged to*
> *him, and he doesn't know how hard it was for me to*
> *have a second abortion. I question whether he loves*
> *me like I love him.*

His phone rang. It was Ashley. "What's up, baby?"

"Where are you? Are you still at Candis's place?"

"Yeah, she's at work, but I'm fixing her garage door.
Everything okay?"

"Hey, will you run by the store and grab something when
you're finished?"

"Sure honey," he said with a little bit of distance in
his voice.

She didn't seem to notice. "Do you mind bringing it so I
can finish cooking? How much longer will you be working?"

"Almost finished," he said. "I'll be there when I'm done."
He just wanted to get her off the phone.

"You're always so available for everyone else, and I ask you to do one thing and your ass acts like you can't. When the hell else would you come? Why do I even ask you to do anything when I know you're gonna make an excuse. Honestly!" She hung up the phone.

"Good," he thought, "Now I can finish this diary." He turned to the middle of the journal:

> *Kevin came over, and we kissed for the first time. It was intense, but I couldn't stop thinking about him. I would have done it, but I didn't want to have sex with Kevin just to get him out of my system.*

Was she talking about Kevin from work? She said she didn't like that motherfucker. "Is she cheating on me?" he thought. "I know she's not messing with me *and* him. I mean, what if I catch something?" He turned a few more pages and learned that, in addition to him, there were several guys she had slept with in the past month. What the fuck? He'd thought she was exclusive with him until he read those passages. He'd been contemplating leaving Ashley, but this made him forget about that quick.

"This motherfucker is trying to play me," he thought.

Then his phone rang again. It was his mom.

"Momma, what's up?"

"It's your brother," she said. "He's in trouble. I may need you to go pick him up."

"Okay, Ma. Just calm down."

Dave

A week earlier, Sydney had called Dave complaining that the man she was living with didn't even notice her.

"Look, suga', where is the guy now?"

"At work," she said.

"Well, he's trying to make a living, and there's only one way to do it. You have to work"

"But I have all this money," Sydney whined.

"Well, does he know that?"

"No. Nobody does but you."

"Well, until you decide to get honest with this guy, he'll continue to work very hard. He sounds like a decent guy who could make an honest woman out of you, girl."

"Yeah… maybe. I met this really hot guy, Jacob, while I was out in Las Vegas, and he made me melt inside. That's the kind of guy I've always wanted. He is so amazing and handsome and beautiful and gentle and kind. Oh, I don't know what

I'm saying." Sydney was rambling in a day-dreamy voice that made Dave interrupt her.

"What do you mean? You don't even know this guy!"

"We had something," she said defensively. "It was something special. I can't really explain it. I've never met anyone in the world like that, and I want it!"

Dave rolled his eyes. "Get yo' life together, girl. Remember what happened with Roman, James, and all the others?"

Sydney smiled. "Yeah, yeah, yeah. Always bringing up old shit. I love you, Dave."

"Love you too, suga'. See you in a few—"

Sydney interrupted. "Nope, I'll be there this weekend."

"Oh really?" Dave's voice was playful.

"Yep, I have to come take care of my Japanese connection. He'll be in town for a conference, and that motherfucker pays handsomely for a backrub and for me to pee on him and other weird shit."

They both laughed. "Hell," she continued, "I may shit on his ass and he'll pay double. He's like, 'Bark like a dog!' But he says it in the weirdest accent. He sounds like the PlayStation commercial. 'Play-Sta-chun!'" She couldn't stop laughing. "Oh my god, I'm fucking the PlayStation guy!"

"Okay, suga'. See you then. Hey, I may need you to take care of something. I'll tell you about it later. Bye love."

"Bye Papa."

Dave hung up the phone, called Jeff, and said, "We are good for this weekend. Just let me know where and when you want it to happen."

"Okay Pop. Thanks for the call. I'm sending the pics to your burner."

Dave pulled up the pictures of the guy. He opened the safe and took out the pistol and silencer. "This young motherfucker thinks he can steal from me and get away with it. I'll take care of his ass this weekend."

Dave's phone rang, and the guy on the other end said, "His name is Marcus Theolona."

"Thanks, partner. Be sure to welcome him with open arms."

"No problem, sir."

Dave deleted the photos and pulled out his cigar. He went to the window and thought about his position in life. Marcus had stolen $5,000 from Dave's Houston connection but didn't know it was Dave's. He thought it was a low-level operation and that he and his buddies were making a quick score. Marcus was just the muscle for the operation and also the only one whose mask was not all the way on. The crew instantly recognized him and sent the information to Dave. Marcus's life was over at that point. Dave was so angry that he almost went down to California to take care of it himself. Had Sydney not unwittingly intervened, Dave would have put himself in the middle of a small street war.

Millie's Diner

There was a huge accident that caused traffic to be backed up for miles. It routed a lot of cars through Millie's Diner, a spot popular with locals on the edge of Vegas. The last of a dying breed, Millie's Diner—an old dark brown and white building on the corner of Red and Oak streets in the middle of town—was a place where people came to relax. It was the last mom and pop restaurant since the neighborhood started turning. A venture capitalist had come into the neighborhood, buying up property to update the city and rid it of undesirables.

First, Mitch and Alex moved their yoga studio to the other side of town; then, Jennifer and Braxton sold their grocery store. Mr. Ballard, the barber, wasn't going anywhere. He was sick of moving after spending twenty-seven years in the army. He'd had enough. "If they think I'm selling my business to a bunch of people who don't give a damn about our community," he'd say, "then they can shit on that shit!"

So he stayed. He always made it to work early and into Millie's Diner for a good cup of coffee and to shoot the breeze with Scoop, an old football teammate from high school. Scoop had a promising career, but influences got the best of him, and he ended up doing a stint in San Quentin.

Mr. Ballard and Scoop were from the old community. They watched as all the youth went off to school and never returned. They'd often discuss the black church as the catalyst for pulling things back together. This particular morning, Mr. Ballard had driven in extra early to play chess with Reverend Sykes. "Main Man," as he called him, had been a drug dealer in high school. He almost hit a mess of trouble until he was saved by the cross. Mr. Ballard, Scoop, and Main Man, along with a few other elders, would meet at Millie's Diner to play spades, dominoes, or chess. They always met in the back, close to the kitchen, so they could shoot the breeze with Scoop— and so he could watch the reverend's cheating ass, as Mr. Ballard put it. Main Man had a mean chess game from playing with so many prisoners, and Mr. Ballard had one from his time in the army. They'd play for hours on end and kept a good conversation going. Everyone knew them, and they knew everyone.

Mr. Ballard said, "You know, Andy, the problem in our community is the church."

To that, Reverend Sykes replied, "Man, I can't get everyone to come to church, let alone fix the problems."

"What about outreach?" asked Mr. Ballard

"Okay, I'm with you there," said the reverend, "But what do you have in mind? We already have homework centers and folks who volunteer, but with all the youth moving out and everyone chasing a dollar, what are we to do?"

"I mean, hell. Look at our own kids. Michelle moved away after attending Fisk and never returned, and Malcolm has no plans to return after he leaves Howard next fall. Their responses are all the same: there's nothing here." Mr. Ballard shook his head.

"Man, I think in our efforts to make a better life for our families, we really forgot about how great this community once was and did not build its future," Scoop hollered from the back. "My boy is gonna be the saving grace of this place. He's giving back to the community and in that ROTC and has plans to go into politics. He might be the motherfucking mayor. Yeah, about to be the godfather of a mayor. Fellas? So you son of a guns have politicians? Yeah, Jack, I didn't think so!"

"You get in them damn grits!" shouted the reverend.

They all laughed.

"Seriously, though, brother. I spoke to Justin just yesterday at the church about how we could get guys from the team to come out and help mentor these youths. That young man is solid." They all agreed.

"We'll continue this later, fellas. I gotta go open up the shop." Scoop started finishing up the bacon for the morning. They agreed to meet again tomorrow, said their goodbyes, and then it got thick in the restaurant.

Scoop was so busy cooking he didn't notice that four hours had passed and there were police crawling all over the restaurant, talking to everyone. He didn't know why everyone was so late for work. He stepped out of the kitchen and thought, "Why are the police out in force? Is it a drug bust? Did some idiot get loose from the cops again?"

Meanwhile, in Millie's dining room, the police were talking to everyone, trying to piece the story together. Scoop walked around and saw some guy at a table with three policemen. He went back to the kitchen and continued to listen from there. Millie, the diner's owner, the one who had given Scoop a second chance, walked in and said, "What's happening, Scoop?"

"Get yo' ass in here, that's what's happening!"

They both laughed, and Millie grumbled, "What the fuck, man? Why are there police all over my damn place? Them motherfuckers better be eating eggs or something. I'll be damned if they running all the paying customers away. Let me git these motherfuckers!"

"Wait, wait," Scoop said quickly. "We just gonna sit in here and listen, and maybe we can find out what happened."

So they both sat in the kitchen, listening to the police. The first thing they heard was Larry.

"They got Larry?" Scoop said. "You know that motherfucker is on probation."

"I know!" Millie whispered. "We might need to call a motherfucker in for his ass because if they run him, his ass is going to jail."

"For sho!" Scoop agreed.

Millie and Scoop listened closely to Larry talking to the police.

"My name is Larry. I work at Millie's. I work in the back. I'm the guy making the burgers. Today started like any normal morning. I got up, got ready, and headed out. I normally work the night shift, but I traded with Donnie last week so I could be off for Cherlyn and I's anniversary. We've been together since high school and…well, every year we like to class it up at the Waffle House because that's where we met. It's always a fun time, and we've been doing it for about ten years now. Cherlyn always orders one pecan waffle to signify our wholeness or something, she said. She's a romantic like that, and it's kinda what I fell in love with if I'm being perfectly honest with you." Larry was nervous; he knew there were warrants out for him, and he tended to be long-winded.

"Oh, well…it's cheap, and cheap ain't bad these days. It was kinda cool out, so I grabbed my jacket, the light jean jacket. Shit, nothing like going back and forth in the freezer all day when it's freezing outside. When I got outside, I realized that it wasn't so bad but still cool enough for the jacket and the sweater I was wearing. Cherlyn bought it for me for one of our anniversaries, so I make it a point to wear it on our anniversary.

"On my way to work, the traffic was smooth. I seemed to catch all the green lights until I got close to the restaurant. At that point, it slowed to a crawl. I tried to see around the cars, but this huge Big Foot monster-looking truck blocked everyone's view. There was a traffic light about a mile up from the restaurant. I noticed a cop directing traffic away from there. I wondered what was going on, but I kinda kept my distance. I was thinking I just don't need to be late again. How am I gonna make it now without Marsha, my supervisor, just having my ass? I was already late twice last week, and she has been riding me since then. I need this fucking shit-ass job so I can keep my PO out of my shit, man. It's honest money, and I get to go home every night. I gave up the life. I'm not stealing anymore, and I'm on track.

"I found a good park on the side of the building in the back—it ended up being perfect. The day was looking up already. I walked around the corner, and there were cops everywhere. Cops with the cop uniforms and then the other kind that wear suits. Detectives? Hell, I don't know what you call them. I walked through the door, and I saw them talking to one guy. I had a few minutes before my shift, so I decided to eavesdrop.

"You want to know what I saw? Well, I was looking out the window. The sun was really bright on my face; it was so bright, I had to put my hand up to block it out. I stood up to pull down the shade when something caught my eye. I looked out the window, and across the street, the scene seemed quite bizarre: two cars parked fairly close to each other. Still running but with no one in them. It all seemed strangely out of place. I mean, it was a normal morning just like the rest. The grass was green, the sun was shining, and people were going to and from, getting on with their days. Folks were coming in and out of this old coffee shop that's been here at least since my mom was a kid and has had only one owner. I looked back out the window and across the street when I noticed two young men. They must have been in their teens or late twenties by the way they were dressed: hooded shirts with long pants falling off at some point and having to be held with their hands. Why wear pants that you have to pull up? One was a slender, handsome, nicer-looking guy, and the other was more of a tough-looking guy. The first guy looked in great shape. The other guy had mass and a toughness about him. Prison strong—you know the look that says he had just gotten out of prison or jail. It wasn't until they got closer that I noticed the cold air blowing from their mouths because it was a little chilly outdoors. The bigger guy looked like he had a gun, too, but I'm not altogether clear on that one, and the young man kept looking behind him as if he was waiting on someone to chase him. Oh, and then the cops pulled up.

"You know what, he did have a gun or something because he dropped it. I bet if we went back there right now, we'd find it. Oh wait…the cops were there, so they probably have it. Once I saw the cops, I felt better, and after the cops left, it didn't really matter to me. I was just about to start my shift. That's all I saw. I tell you what, if you guys talk to the people in the building across the street, you may get more information. There was a lady staring out the window up there on the third floor. I bet she saw everything. She has a better view anyway."

The police made their way across the street to speak with the lady on the third floor. She explained, "I did hear the craziest noise, and it woke me up out of my sleep. I immediately jumped up to see what it was and to check on my little furry friend. I always feed this cat. I named him Francisco. He's the loveliest little guy. Gray hair, furry, and downright adorable. He's not a fan of the milk or all the noise that I make, but he's there everyday. He comes around when I'm ironing and getting ready for work most nights. It started one night when I went to throw out some chicken bones. I thought I saw ants on the mantel, and before I knew it, I had thrown them out of the window. Francisco immediately ran over and started eating. It made me feel better because I hate to litter. After that, every night he comes at the same time, sits on the landing, and so I just started fixing him a plate after dinner and running it down. It's to the point where he just sleeps in the alley now. He and I both sleep during the days because I work nights.

"Forgive me for being a bit long, but I really like the cat, and I want to bring him in. But the super doesn't allow pets in this place. Nevertheless, the noise. I looked out the window to check on what it was, getting up to throw on my robe because most days I sleep with the window open, but I'm not a fan of pervs. You get the picture. I see these two guys running and ducking behind the hotel. Then, not even three minutes later, I hear more guys running, but these guys were bigger. Thug guys, you know, the bad kind you see in the movies. All rough-you-up kind of guys. Oh, and they were, well, ya know, urban. I immediately picked up the phone to call the cops. They said they would be there right away.

"There's a homeless guy who lives back there. I see him every day. He's a really nice guy, and he has the perfect view from his box. You should try him, and I'd bet you get a better view of things."

After the police finished talking to the lady, they went downstairs to find the homeless man behind the hotel. He was asleep when they walked up and was immediately startled by the two police officers. He grabbed his things because he assumed he was getting kicked out of the alley. They stopped him and explained that they had questions about the incident. With relief in his eyes, he put his things away and began to explain to the police what he saw:

"I was in the dumpster behind the restaurant, looking for breakfast. You can get some good shit in there, man. Hell, last week I found a steak that still had the sauce on it. I tore that shit up. I felt like I was dining at a fine restaurant. Oh, and I also had a piece of cake. I think it was red velvet. It's funny the shit people throw away. I saw these two dudes, man, running as I was about to hop out the dumpster. They didn't really see me; homeless folks are kinda invisible to y'all motherfuckers anyway. But, like I was saying, one of the motherfuckers stepped on my bed and mashed up my newspaper. I was about to say, 'Watch where you' goin'

sorry asshole!' Until I saw the gun. Hey, I ain't no damn
fool, man. I don't know why the hell they back here running
anyway, but whatever it was, I didn't want no part of it.
Normally back here all you see are hookers and johns doin'
their thang. Actually, that's why I picked this spot because
I know that I could probably get me a few dollars to watch
out for the cops. It's a good side hustle, you know. Like I
said, though, when I saw the gun, I was like whoa. I ducked
down a bit and waited them out. It was crazy, man."

Justin

No. This is not the way. Don't do it like this, man. Let's go, dude. Come on!" Justin pleaded as they sat in a car outside of an old apartment complex on the other side of town. "Think about lil' Necy and Shea-shea. They don't deserve this shit, man."

Necy and Shea-shea were Marcus's two kids that he had by two different women. If he couldn't play ball, Justin didn't know what he would do to support them.

"Thanks, brother, but this is happening today. If you want to bounce, I understand. I know you gotta go support your mom. It's cool, man. I'm a be here, and I'm gonna get these motherfuckers. As a matter of fact, just hand me your ammo and you go ahead and dip. You've always been my ride-or-die homeboy, but I don't want this to fall back on you, man. You've got your whole life ahead of you."

Just then, Justin got a text from his mom: "I need you to run by the bank for me and grab us some cash for tonight's party. We'll need about $500 to make change for the bar."

He typed back quickly: "Ok Mom. I'll be there."

He had completely forgotten about the party and that he'd promised to help his mom with the bar. Thirty minutes passed as they sat there in the parking lot. "Is this really what they came here for?" Justin thought as the minutes ticked by. "Do we really want to kill the guy?"

Marcus was dead set on avenging their friend Peanut and the rest of the crew who'd been shot by these thugs. They were at a party on the side of town with burglar-barred windows and liquor stores on every corner. Great parties happened over there, but a motherfucker might get shot in the process. On that particular day, Peanut and the crew had just arrived. They walked in, greeting, dapping everyone up, hugging, and exchanging pleasantries. The first shots rang out, but they were down the street, and since something was always poppin' off, they kept the party going. The party was great, and the girls were looking right—at least that what the guys thought. Peanut could not stop thinking about Venesia. He pulled her to the side of the house and immediately started giving her his best lines.

"Come on, baby. You know we been trying to get together since last year, but either you were with someone or I was with someone."

"That's true," she said with her southern Mississippi accent.

"So what's up now? We are both unattached—as if it was meant for us to be together." He moved in closer, smiling, looking into her eyes.

She smiled back, then looked away and said, "But you kinda dangerous and run with the wrong crowd. I don't want to be running all the time. Or getting shot at."

"I'll change everything for you. I'm looking to wife you, girl. Just give me time to show you I've changed my ways, and we can work this out."

Venesia really liked Peanut. She always had, but her friends had warned her to stay away from him. Peanut was a major gang banger and trouble followed him. He was the kind of guy who shot first and asked questions later. But she wanted to jump in with both feet and not look back. She was ready to take this journey with him. She smiled. He smiled back and pulled her closer. She leaned up for a kiss. "Done!" he thought.

"Let me go get you something to drink," he said with a big smile. He was overwhelmed with joy. He started to walk away, lifting her hand and kissing it as he went.

"Hennessy straight," she said.

Almost immediately, a black Crown Victoria with crisp paint and a fresh wash drove past. The music was thumping with some local rap that shook the party and made everyone stop and look. The car slowed down, and Peanut yelled, "Guns! Get down! Venesia!" He took the first shot in the leg and another in the back. Before he could get to her, he watched Venesia take a shot in the jaw and another in her arm. They were sprayed with machine guns, and a lot of the folks at the party were hit. In total, seven of the thirty or so people there were shot by these guys.

Marcus and Justin had left the party to do a beer run and grab two girls who'd been showing major interest in them.

Marcus got a call about the shooting while he was pumping gas. He ran into the store to grab Justin. "We gotta bounce, dude!"

Justin saw the anger in Marcus's eyes and knew something bad had gone down. Once they were on the road, Marcus explained that Peanut and some of the others were hit. Paramedics were on the scene. The girls wanted to help, but Marcus dropped them off back in their neighborhood.

Marcus was furious. He'd had a run-in with the guys who did the shooting and felt horrible that his friend Peanut took a bullet that was meant for him. "Shit, man. I should have been there. Those shots were meant for me."

"Don't say that, brother," Justin said. "They were just being reckless and not trying to hit anybody. Just fucking with us."

"You call this fucking with us?" Marcus snapped. "Them motherfuckers did this on purpose, man. We need to handle this shit today! Those are the same weak-ass bitches I got into it with at the game last week. I knew I should have aced his ass, but the cops were around, and I'm on probation already over that dumb shit from last year."

He was referring to beating up an off-duty security guard for bumping into him and not saying excuse me. Marcus was always getting involved in trivial pursuits and chasing the ghost of his father not being around. He never dealt with the pent-up aggression, and it was always ready to boil over. The only time it was tamed was on the football field, where he excelled and where that aggression was an asset to the team. He was big, fast, and angry—the best combination for an outside lineman whose job was to sack the quarterback. He was so good, in fact, that he was heavily recruited even though he was on probation, but he'd decided to go with a local team to stay close to his friends.

Justin had wanted to get away, but he received a nice package from the local school, making going anywhere else difficult to justify. As a result, the two of them were in it together. The coaches had several people watching Marcus to keep him out of trouble. Unbeknownst to Justin was the fact that he was recruited partly for that purpose, to assist in keeping their star outside linebacker out of trouble.

Marcus was remorseful about not dealing with the guy in the Crown Victoria last week, right after their argument. "Damn, how could I be so stupid?" he said. "Now they got my boy on a motherfucking stretcher over some shit I did. Oh, it's on. That motherfucker tried me! Let's go get these fools!"

Marcus rode to a house Justin didn't recognize. It had white burglar bars on the windows and doors. The grass was overgrown, and several guys were hanging outside. There were cars parked in the grass, and one guy in a wheelchair was smoking a cigarette out front when they arrived. His name was Eddie. He lost his legs in a car accident, but it only made him more of a thug. Marcus jumped out of the car and said to Justin, "Wait here, man. I need to grab something."

Justin was angry about what had happened but didn't like how Marcus was reacting to the situation. He could normally talk Marcus out of crazy plans, but this was different. This was the first time that something Marcus did had come back on his friends. He was furious. Marcus came out of the house with a big black bag. Justin looked at him and committed to the plan with a nod—despite his serious doubts.

And now they were sitting in a parking lot, minutes away from attempting murder.

Justin was even less enthusiastic about the whole idea because he was on an ROTC scholarship. He had one foot in and one out of the hood. His uncle had convinced him that military life was the way to go. He'd bought into it and joined the ROTC. He thought, "Damn, I should not be in this car. We have guns, AK-47s, and all sorts of knives. What the fuck am I doing?" All because this Marcus wanted to get back at somebody? Was he really sitting here risking ass rape if caught because someone wanted to get back at another guy? He wondered if Big Bubba would take it easy on him in the cell. He wondered if he'd be thinking about this very moment as he was doing the unspeakable.

After about an hour of waiting, Marcus finally said, "You're right, man. Fuck it, let's go! Them motherfuckers ain't showing!"

"You sure, man?" Justin said, not revealing how relieved he was.

Marcus nodded.

Now, Justin could go get with the hottie from the bar. She was round and plump—just like he liked it—with reddish blond hair and a wonderful wit. She reminded him of all the girlfriends from every chick flick he'd ever watched. "Well, Bubba, you'll have to wait, my friend," he said to himself.

"What are you talking about, man?" asked Marcus.

"Never mind." Justin let out a sigh of relief.

Bang! Crack! Smash! Screech!

"Fuck, what was that?"

"Someone just sideswiped us!" Marcus exclaimed, agitated again. He started to pull over when he realized that the other car was not stopping. "Are you fucking kidding me? A hit and run? Today of all days? Okay motherfuckers! It's on!" Marcus pressed the gas pedal all the way down and started to give chase.

Justin was thinking he had spoken too soon. Bubba might just get one more crack at his ass.

They chased the guys for about seven blocks and into an alley, where they jumped out of the car and started chasing them on foot. Justin took off first. He was built like a distance runner but had wheels for speed. He always placed in the top five at every state meet.

Marcus was built like a lineman, six-five and 285 pounds. He ran like a snail compared to Justin. By the time he could say, "Wait up, man!" Justin was down the block.

They were after two guys with black gear and a bag. The guys were small; they looked Nepalese. Justin thought it was strange these guys were so far from home. He had almost caught up to them, but then they disappeared. "Where the fuck did they go?" he wondered. "And so fast?"

Marcus showed up and couldn't believe the madness. Out of breath, he asked, "Where...du'...dude. Where are they?

Justin shook his head. They did a quick search and started to walk off. "Fuck!" Marcus screamed, "You don't fuckin' do a hit and run on me motherfuckers! It ain't over!"

They didn't hear the two guys talking behind the hotel. The two guys figured Justin and Marcus were undercover cops from the deal that had just gone bad. As they stood there looking out the window, they started to discuss their plans.

"We need to split up! They'll be looking for two guys with a bag," Hector said. "Keep the dope. I'll come get it from you later. I've got to get home, man. She's gonna fuckin kill me if I'm late."

"Okay, later bro."

Hector took off out the front door of the hotel, caught a cab, and headed home.

Marcus and Justin started walking back to the car when Justin got a text from Julia, the hottie from the bar. She wanted to meet up later. His excitement level went back up. Tonight was her night off, and she wanted to spend it with him.

"It's her, man! She wants to give yo' boy some time tonight!"

"You mean some head? Guts? Snatch? Pitch and catch?" Marcus said. He gave his friend a high five, and they laughed it up. "Man, now I gotta find me one."

"What about the girl from Denny's?" asked Justin.

"She does have a fat ass!" Marcus grinned. As they came out of the alley, they noticed the police looking around the car.

"Get rid of that damn gun, man!" Justin hissed.

"Shit. This day, man!" Marcus threw the gun in the trash. He then walked over to his car, and addressed the two police officers looking in the window. "Excuse me, officers. Is there a problem?"

"No, son. It just seems as if someone got the best of this car. Is it yours?"

"Yeah, my fucking sister, man. She can't drive for shit."

The officer smiled and said, "I definitely understand that. Been trying to teach my little girl to drive, and we've had our share of challenges. Are you guys okay? You seem flushed."

Justin jumped in. "This motherfucker thought he could beat me in a race, but as you can see, his sweaty ass didn't win."

They all let out a laugh, exchanged pleasantries, and headed on their separate ways. The officers looked back and one said, "Look, guys, it's nice to have fun. Just be careful out here." The policemen got in their car and took off.

Marcus was surprised they didn't recognize him since he was one of the biggest stars in the land. He was actually pretty bummed about it.

Justin was feeling good. He looked up at the sun and saw there were about fourteen minutes of daylight remaining. He was always into science as a kid and knew how to tell time by looking at the sun. "Funny the shit you remember from eighth grade," he thought. He reflected on the events of the day and gave a big finger to the sky. "Testing me today, huh big guy?" he asked out loud.

They were about to get into the car when someone started yelling Marcus's name from across the street. He looked up and said, "Wait, that looks like Sydney."

"Who the fuck is Sydney?" asked Justin

"Only the finest motherfucker to ever work at Food Lion," Marcus laughed.

As he was about to walk over, she disappeared, but as she did, they noticed a beautiful woman walking up to them. Marcus saw her first and instantly thought God had answered his prayers. She looked like she stepped right out of a Victoria's Secret catalogue. Very exotic, possibly Asian and black—or even white. The way the sun was shining from behind her, it wasn't easy to tell. The parts of her that were undeniable were the hips and butt. She wore black running shoes with a body-hugging dress. She smiled, and it was the warmest and most familiar smile Marcus had seen in awhile. Justin thought she seemed out of place, but they were too focused on her striking good looks and voluptuous body to care.

It was also odd that she had on running shoes with her dress, but she got a pass because she was absolutely gorgeous. She looked at Marcus and said, "Hi."

He was so excited he could barely muster a return greeting. She was beautiful, and in Marcus's mind, he was already making plans for later. He thanked God so many times between the introduction that he lost count.

"Are you Marcus Theleona, the football player?" she asked.

"Yes ma'am. Always nice to see fans."

"You probably don't remember me," she continued with an uncomfortable smile. "You were pretty wasted. I've been looking all over for you. It's so nice to finally see you again."

Marcus looked bewildered. He had slept with many women provided by boosters and other sponsors, but he was not placing this girl.

"You are much more handsome than I remember," she said, stepping closer. She seemed to have her hand on her purse, but Marcus didn't really notice.

Suddenly he remembered her face. "You're the girl from the bar."

"That's right," she said, and her voice cracked.

"We damn sure had a good time, didn't we?"

Justin climbed in the car, leaving the two of them talk. Marcus moved closer and said, "Look, I'm sorry for what happened. I didn't mean anything by it."

"I'm sorry, too. I probably will never be the same again." Her eyes started to swell with tears, and Marcus bent down to hug her.

"Don't touch me, motherfucker!" she snapped, and before she knew it, she had taken the gun out of her purse and shot him in the head. Marcus fell to the sidewalk, and she stepped over him. "You won't rape anyone else now."

She didn't look back at Justin as she walked away.

Justin jumped out of the car, stunned. He and Marcus had known each other since they were four years old. The woman casually walked across the street. A black coupe pulled up—she just hopped in and took off.

"What the fuck just happened?"

Justin felt completely responsible for what had happened to Marcus. If only he had stood up to him and made him think through the consequences of his actions, they wouldn't be in this predicament. And now his friend lay dead in his arms. That was the damn girl from the other night? Who the fuck was Sydney, and why did it look like that damn girl got into the car with her? Justin had a lot of unanswered questions and wasn't going to stop until he had answers.

Justin couldn't believe what he had just witnessed and didn't know what to do going forward. He tried to remember the license plate number, but it was all a blur. The girl looked like she wore a wig—was it brown with purple highlights? She didn't look to be from around this area.

He grabbed his iPhone and dialed 911. He explained the situation and begged them to get there quickly. His phone was buzzing as Julia kept texting, but he didn't have the energy to text her back. He sat there holding his friend and waiting for the ambulance. The police arrived and immediately started administering aid.

"There's a pulse," one guy said as he directed Justin to keep his hand on the wound.

An older officer walked up and said, "It's going to be okay, son. The paramedics are here, and if there's anything to do, they will do it." Marcus died on the way to the hospital.

Justin began to cry. They wanted descriptions of the shooter and details about why they were there. Everyone knew Marcus Theolona, so it wasn't long before the news cameras arrived on the scene. California's own Marcus Theolona was gunned down in cold blood. It would be the saddest story on the news for months, and police departments would vie to get to the bottom of who had done the killing. The mayor got on TV exclaiming how this violence needed to stop. Churches prayed on the scene for a week or so, and a makeshift shrine sprung up at the site. Marcus's family pleaded with the public to stop all the drugs and black-on-black crime.

At his funeral, his mom asked, "Why do we keep killing each other? Aren't we tired of this? I lost my son. No other mother should have to go through this. This is no way to live. We are not meant to bury our children. God did not intend for this to happen, but I know that it is His will, and I won't question it. But right now...right now, in this moment..." Her eyes swelled with tears. "Lord, I just don't understand it!"

Marcus's mom had to be ushered to her seat. Linda patted her arm and stood up to finish what she had started: "Marcus was a wonderful young man," she said, her voice strong. "We are all proud to have had him in our homes, our lives, and around our children. He made us a community. He gave us all something to cheer for and put us on the map. We will always honor his memory. I ask you to keep Marcus in your memories and keep him with you as we continue to make a difference in this world. Barbara, don't worry. We will continue to walk with you because none of us knows how difficult it is to lose a child. You are our family. Marcus was our family. We are all family. I know that Justin and the rest of his teammates, friends, and loved ones are hurting, but Marcus lived life. Let's learn from his example and know God got an angel early."

Linda finished her speech, and there wasn't a dry eye in the room. Marcus's funeral had the look of a dignitary's. The mayor, state representatives, the chief of police, coaches, and players from other teams were there, all arm in arm. His death brought the community closer together.

The football team dedicated its year to Marcus and his memory; players even wore black tape on their uniforms and wrists. Each wore the number 18—Marcus's number—on their helmets to symbolize unity. It was a nice gesture, and it temporarily brought the city together. The police came up with dry holes, and the murderer was never found, even though the shooting happened in daylight in front of an eyewitness. The chief of police was pissed at his stack of unsolved murders, but he didn't have the staff or the budget to do anything about it.

"Add this one to the pile," he said with disgust. "We have to get better about this."

Justin couldn't quite get over it. The sadness was overwhelming, and in some way, he knew it had changed him forever.

The chief made one last phone call to his first cousin: "Louie."

"What's up, Chief?"

"You know what went down, don't you?"

"Drug deal gone bad as far as I'm concerned."

"I need more than that, man. These guys are on my ass and pressing me to do more."

"Give me some time," Louie said. "I'll get you something."

Bianca received a text from Dave that said: "You've got to get out of town tonight." She quickly grabbed her things and ran back to the hotel. Sydney was waiting with a bag to take her to the airport. She dropped the girl off and quickly realized that Bianca had left her cellphone. She jumped out of the car to take it back to her, but a guy grabbed her arm. He said he was an undercover ATF agent who had been watching them for years.

"Let me go, you sick fuck!" She screamed and reached in her bag for her revolver.

"Either come with me now or you are going to jail," the guy said. "And you won't see Lance or Junior ever again."

Then she saw the black car behind her. It had flashing lights and seemed legit. She took her hand off the weapon, and the guy dropped her in his car and jumped in the driver's seat.

A short while later, Sydney sat in a Spartan cell in handcuffs trying to determine what to do with all the information in her head. She had a huge decision to make: turn on Dave or go to jail. Dave had always been so kind to her, and she couldn't believe that his own cousin had double-crossed him. "I just dropped that bitch off at the airport," she thought.

The door to the cell opened. "You're free to go now, Miss."

She ran outside to the black limo waiting in the parking lot. Dave wanted to make sure she was okay. He'd been tipped off by one of his friends that the police had taken Sydney. He also heard about Marcus but couldn't react because he knew someone in his camp was snitching. He wasn't sure that it wasn't Sydney; he didn't think it was, but he had to be sure.

"Dave!" She was relieved he had picked her up himself so she could tell him about his cousin. He sent a quick text to one of his people, and within days, Bianca was gone. No one could find her.

This whole mess was all a ploy to take Dave down. Was it all planned? Sydney wondered who else was in on it. Lance? She called him, and he immediately sensed the tension in her voice.

"Is everything okay, love?" he asked.

"Umm, sure," she said with half-hearted lightness in her voice. "But there's something going on. I can't really explain, but I need you and Junior to come to Vegas right now. Leave your cellphone and everything you have and meet me on the highway. I'll be in a black SUV. I'm tracking you—my car has a GPS tracker on it. I can explain when you get here, but someone may come to the house looking for me, and they don't need to find you there alone with the baby. You're not safe."

"What do you want me to do about the money?" he asked.

"Bring it, but be careful. It's a lot. Just be careful, baby."

Dave went to his hideaway to let the storm blow over. If the cops were after Sydney, it meant the snitch in his organization was closer to him than he thought. He called a meeting of all his lieutenants to narrow down the search. He had a hunch it was Peter Vinkler, a former cellmate of his, but had no proof. A police officer had told him once that Peter was jealous and power hungry.

Dave brought Peter to the office and straight-up asked if he was the guy.

"Are you fucking kidding me? Why would I do that?"

Dave saw something, and it was enough. He stood and shot Peter square in the chest. "Fuckin' narc," he said. "Somebody clean this shit up."

Then he just turned and walked away.

Dave

Bianca was ready to get on her plane and never look back. She was sorry for turning on Dave, and the fact that she had blood on her hands only made matters worse. She was responsible for the takedown of one of the most powerful figures in Vegas. The ATF had him on extortion charges and couldn't wait to throw the book at him.

She loved Dave, but she could never forget the stories she'd heard about how he had killed her dad. When she was younger, she knew her dad's life had suddenly been taken from him, but she never knew by whom or why. Those were questions that burned inside her every day. She'd been close to her dad as a child. She was Daddy's little girl; she meant the world to him, and to her he was the moon. He was always there, looking over his "baby girl." When she was younger, her big cousin Dixie would come over and stay the night, just like all the cousins did. Her house was fun, and her parents had a little money so they had cable and all the good snacks. Her father, Joe, was a heavy drinker but not enough to be considered an alcoholic. His favorite was an ice cold forty of Old English. He would always send baby girl to the icebox to grab one for him, and when she came back with it, he presented her with a dollar. She loved her daddy. She would do anything for him.

One evening, there was a big slumber party at her house for her birthday. All the kids were running around inside and outside, and all her uncles, aunts, and cousins were in attendance. The adults were in the backyard with the barbecue, and the kids were in the house playing Nintendo and watching movies on separate TVs. A few hours had passed, and it was getting late. The adults started to leave one by one, but the kids would stay the night and finish celebrating her birthday. She was ecstatic. This was one of those days when her daddy had worked really hard to make sure the food was perfect, the yard looked nice, and everyone was having a good time. Bianca's mom had made her a cake shaped like a flower. It was a beautiful pink cake with a yellow center. You would have thought it was a store-bought cake; baking was her mom's thing. Because her dad had spent all day getting things together, he started drinking once the people arrived. He was drinking a forty every two hours. He was way over his limit.

Dixie had always taken a liking to Joe. To her, Uncle Joe was cool. That night, when all the adults had gone and the kids were playing in Bianca's room, Dixie went down to the basement, where Uncle Joe was listening to music.

She knew that was where she could find him. Joe had a pretty decent radio system in the basement, and he had an infectious love for the blues that rubbed off on Dixie. Dixie went over to the couch and sat next to her uncle. They listened to a few songs, and then Joe told Dixie to get up and dance. Folks were always telling children to get up and dance, and they did so even if they didn't want to. The rule was that if you were a child, you were for entertainment purposes. So Dixie did as she was told and danced, acting out some of the new dance moves she'd seen her mom and dad do at home. Once the song finished, she sat down next to Joe again. But Joe grabbed Dixie's face and, with slurred speech, said, "You're a pretty little girl, you know that?"

Dixie just laughed. She knew her uncle was under the influence, and she'd never been called a "pretty" before. Then Joe pulled Dixie's face closer and kissed her. Dixie had been kissed by her aunts and uncles before, so she thought nothing of it.

The next thing Dixie knew, she was stripped naked, and Joe was playing in her panties. It did not feel right to her but she didn't really know what to say or do, this was her favorite Uncle. She knew something wasn't right, but it was Uncle Joe. Uncle Joe was cool. he wouldn't do anything wrong. He wouldn't hurt his favorite niece, would he? After that night, similar attempted assaults happened maybe four more times over the years. It went on until Dixie was old enough to understand that it should not be happening between an uncle and his niece.

Dixie was crying one day when her cousin Stephen found her. Stephen was the one everyone thought was "different," but he was really close to Dixie.

Dixie always felt different from the other kids and didn't quite identify with being a girl. She would remark to Stephen that she often felt like a man trapped in a woman's body. She lived a fast life and played softball, volleyball, and basketball. Dixie was eighteen when she received an offer to attend Stanford on a volleyball, basketball, or softball scholarship—her choice. She elected to forego college and move out to the big city: Las Vegas. She felt that was the only place where she could be accepted for who she was; where she could finally transition into Dave.

Life in Las Vegas moved fast, and she continued to grow into Dave. She met a few friends and started dating a prominent member of the violent community who showed her the ropes. Dave took over the business after his lover died. He was even more ruthless and unforgiving, and he quickly became the most feared man in Vegas. He had cops, legislators, and many other prominent members of society on his payroll. Nothing happened in Vegas without him knowing about it.

Dave knew the feds were on to him, but he didn't have the particulars. He needed them to get close enough so he could sniff out the rat. Once he figured out who was doing all of the digging, he sent a few thugs after him to clean him up and make him back off. The guy wouldn't budge; he was a hard ass from the old school looking to settle scores and was tired of ruthless thugs like Dave and his ilk. He'd been a real fan of Marcus's and had met with Justin immediately after the murder. Justin was too upset to talk, but the guy gave him a card and told him he'd follow up in a few weeks. He was determined to take down Dave and would not rest until it happened.

A month passed before the investigator's phone rang. It was Justin.

"Hey, Mr. Jackson," Justin said. "We need to talk. I have something that might be helpful to the investigation. Can we meet soon?"

"Of course," Jackson said. "Come by the office and we can talk."

"I'm on my way."

Candis

Candis was sitting at her desk at home finishing up some bills and watching the Christmas Day parade on TV when her man called.

"Hey, what's up?" he said. "What are you doing?"

"Working, silly. Wrapping up these bills. What's up? What time does your plane land?"

"I'll be there around 4:00," he said. "I'm bringing you the sweater you left on the nightstand. It's kind of missing its owner, and besides, it doesn't look right on me."

She smiled. "Yeah, your cleavage doesn't do the sweater any justice. You need these babies right here: Juicy and Fruit." She grabbed her boobs, looking in the mirror and grinning.

They laughed and enjoyed a few moments talking about what was about to be one of the best weekends they'd had in a long time.

They always had a good time. The last time they were together, they flew to New Orleans on a whim. They were driving past the airport when he asked, "Hey, have you ever been to a crawfish boil?"

When she said no, he pulled up the Delta app on his phone and booked two first-class tickets to the Big Easy. Candis remembered thinking that she had never experienced anything like this man. He was so together and had so many talents and was so much fun. He was the most intelligent man she had ever met.

The night before he was expected to arrive, she stayed up all night cleaning her place. She wanted everything to be right for him. He was her man, and she wanted to make him feel special. She laid out his robe on the chair in the corner of the room because he seemed to like that spot, even though it drove her a little nuts. She was very particular about everything in her house. Candis thought, "There's a place for everything, and everything has its place." Except for his stuff.

She bought his favorite meal: Cornish hen, potatoes, and asparagus. She bought two bottles of wine and his beloved Crown Royal. "Oh, I better not forget the Coke," she thought. "He might have a stroke." Then she let out a laugh.

She started mentally going through her checklist: "Sheets washed, check. Dinner made, check. New panties with the bow on them, check." She continued through her list and decided to lie down on the bed and wait for his call. She woke up to her cellphone ringing.

"Hey, you up?"

"Yeah, what's up?"

"My flight may be delayed a bit."

"How delayed?" Candis was slightly agitated.

"Hell, you sound asleep anyway. What were you doing?" He was trying to lighten the mood.

"Don't worry about what's going on over here. How delayed?"

"Just long enough to finish the meeting. We have another project to tackle, and it may take longer than expected. You know how slow Dexter's ass is about decisions, and we're pitching to him today. We need this money, so they want me here." He sounded tired.

She smiled, thinking how proud she was to have such a smart, hardworking man. "Baby, go in there and kill it. Take your time because I am so ready for you, and when you do arrive, I need you to be here completely with me. I'm wet just thinking about it." That gave him the boost he didn't know he needed. She immediately thought about the rest of their lives and how perfect it would be if he moved closer.

Now that he would be late, she decided to catch up on a few things at the office. It was only around 9:30 a.m., and she figured she could pull off almost a full day of work. She made herself up for the office and decided to wear the heels with the black straps across the front that he loved so much. He called those her come fuck me pumps. She always smiled when she thought of him. Almost everything she did these days had him in mind, and she loved it. She loved him.

When she walked into the building, the security guard gave her so much attention that she often wondered if he ever watched anything besides her ass. "Good morning, Miss Candis," he said, looking her up and down in that creepy way that made her think she better never walk to her car at night around him.

"Morning," she responded in the coldest way possible, putting her keys and change on the belt and walking through the metal detector. She made a mental note not to ever wear any metal to work: "I don't need that pervert's hands all over my shit. Sorry brother, this ass is reserved for someone else!"

She walked into the office, and everyone asked why she was hanging out at work on her day off. She explained that she needed to finish a few things and then she was off.

"I love your new hairstyle," said Kevin. He was so sincere with his compliments. Everyone thought they would make a perfect match. Linda said so. Her BFF Gail agreed. Hell, even the lady at the local deli asked why Candis didn't snatch Kevin up. She thought he would probably make some girl a good husband, but not her. He was always so nice but kind of clingy.

"Yeah, thanks for noticing Kevin." She wanted to beat him to the punch before he asked her out, so she added, "I'm just closing out a few things before the long weekend because I have to go help my parents and grandparents with a few baby shower things for my cousin."

She said this with all the confidence you needed to sell a bold-faced lie. Still couldn't believe that she had stooped to the level of making out with him. His body language made it clear that they didn't share the same impression of their relationship. She wasn't interested in him, but she had obviously given him a false impression.

"How about you, Kevin?" she said lightly.

"Oh, you know. Just gonna brush up on my Spanish and taekwondo, and I might catch a movie. If you're free…"

"Sorry Kev," she interrupted. "This is a horrible weekend. Maybe some other time."

He looked at her with a half-hearted grin. "Okay, sure. Some other time."

As he started to walk off, he mumbled, "Well, umm… you…have a good time."

"Thanks! You too!"

Candis needed to close out her major client files for the week because she didn't want the phone to ring at all once he made it to town. She was a detailed planner and very anal about her time and resources. She planned it so that she'd get in a few hours of work, head to the airport, grab a coffee, heat up their dinner, and be sipping wine and enjoying him by 7:00 p.m.

She couldn't think about anything else, and it was getting her worked up. That was her state when Gail called: "Girl, what are you up to? Are you ready? Are you excited to see your man this weekend? Why don't we go to lunch and you can tell me everything?"

Gail was her best friend from work and had always been supportive. She gave her the first trivet she'd ever owned when she moved into her apartment. It was custom made with a big "C" on it. Candis always thought it was the sweetest gift and liked Gail a lot after that.

"No, girl. I gotta close out these clients. I'll catch up with you on the backside."

"Okay then. Keep me posted." Gail hung up the phone.

Her phone buzzed with texts. She kept picking it up thinking it was him, but it was Jamal, her onetime friend with benefits from college. She had found out through a mutual friend that he was back in town. He wanted to run up on a booty call, but she was all called out. She had no time for him, and he couldn't compete with the love she had for her man, anyway. It's amazing how we go from lust, to love, to annoyed.

She finished up her last e-mail and said, "Done. Focused!"

She headed for the airport, about a twenty minute drive, and decided to stop for gas and grab a cup of coffee on her way. As she was pouring her coffee, she got a little on the arm of her blue blouse. It really irritated her, but she was too focused on what was about to happen to get too worked up.

It had been three months since they last saw each other, and the way they'd left things only made them more eager for the next time. There was so much passion between them, and it built every time they saw each other.

The last time, they had fallen asleep on the floor. The thought of it made her smile, and she wanted to jump right into it. He couldn't get to town fast enough.

She pulled up to the airport cellphone lot about ten minutes early for flight 1862 from Chicago. But then she got a text: "Delayed. Missed that one."

Her face turned red. She was livid.

"WTF?" she texted back.

The phone rang. "Babe?"

"What?"

"I need you to park the car and get on flight 678 to Chicago. I already booked your ticket. I'll be there waiting when you get off."

"Wait. What?" she said. "What about my clothes? Toiletries?" He'd completely changed the plan in the blink of an eye.

"Don't worry, we can get that. I just want to see you. The plane is ready and waiting on you. I just called in a favor, so you have exactly fifteen minutes to get through the line and to the flight. It should be quick because you don't have bags." He said it with all the confidence that she loved about him.

She was antsy but also excited and boarded the flight to Chicago.

She was beyond excited when she deplaned. Coming down the escalator, she saw it: his beautiful white smile and adorable brown eyes. He was super confident, built like a track star with the brains of a genius. She loved everything about him. He was the man of her dreams, and she was the woman of his dreams. They always shared the warmest embrace.

"You are crazy!" she said with a big smile on her face.

He looked at her with that confident grin and gestured with his hands up in the air as if to say, "What are you gonna do?" Then they embraced. She never wanted it to end.

Justin

Justin arrived at the investigator's office around three o'clock in the afternoon. He was familiar with the area. It was adjacent to the hotel where his mom's company held its annual ball. He walked into the large building confident in the investigator's abilities. The guy seemed legit. He knew Marcus, and he would come to their games. He even went out of his way to reach out to Justin, which was promising.

Justin got off the elevator and headed down the hall to the second door on the left. It was a wide corridor, and as he walked, he could feel his heart beating fast. He could barely focus on the many passersby.

"Welcome Justin," the investigator said as Justin walked through the door. The man rose to shake his hand. "What can I do for you, young man? I'm really sorry again about our friend Marcus."

"Yeah me too," Justin said. "But let me cut to the chase. Before Marcus was shot, he spoke to some girl named

Sydney Roundtree. She was coming out of the diner across the street where we were parked. He said they were very familiar and went back quite a ways. She was with some guy, and the girl who shot Marcus got into the car with them. I believe that would be a good start. I'm sorry it took me so long to get back to you, but I've been having a tough time dealing with all this."

"It's quite all right, son. That's very helpful. I'll follow up with a few leads. Thank you for coming in to meet with me. Is there anything else I can do for you?"

Justin stood up to shake the investigator's hand again. He'd been fighting tears since he walked in the door, and he finally broke. "Sorry, sir." His voice shook as he wiped his eyes. The two men embraced.

"Don't worry, son. We will make this right."

Sydney

Three months earlier…

Jacob unpacked and headed to the bar. He thought the hotel had a nice atmosphere with its tall ceilings and wide-open entrance. The place was alive and packed with women. Out of the corner of his eye, he spotted something very small in the distance and approached carefully. "Is that a midget?" he thought. "I've never seen one of them outside the circus." As he walked by, he confirmed that it was, indeed, a midget.

"Bitch, keep your hands off me before I fuck you up!" the little person snapped. There were two girls standing around the lady, trying to pat her head. They thought it was funny.

Jacob quickly got out of their way and went back to soaking up the scene at the hotel. The number of blackjack tables blew his mind.

He was thinking he could have stayed down the hall for cheaper, but his AMEX business travel card was able to score his suite at the Bellagio on short notice. "Platinum status, baby!" he thought as he ordered his first drink. "Yeah, Dad, keep your coins. I got this!"

The platinum AMEX card had all the benefits he'd heard about. First, it was the airport lounge, then the car rental at Hertz, and now the hotel. To top it all off, the company was paying for it, too. "Winning!" he said softly. He was on a high and was going to ride it out while he waited on his friends. He walked around the hotel for a bit and decided to hang out at the bar.

He was there for a conference that coincided with Nick and JC's wedding. He was one of the groomsman, and though he wasn't totally comfortable with their union, Nick had been his buddy since college, and well, he didn't want to be all homophobic. "Besides," he thought, "more ass for me!"

He sat there scouting out this blond hottie from across the room wearing a blue, low-cut dress with black heels. They were eye flirting when he heard a voice next to him. "Excuse me, is this seat taken?" a woman asked, quickly sizing him up. He was tall enough, cute enough. Sure, she'd give him a chance.

"No, please have a seat," he said. He thought that this couldn't have been any easier. This chick made the blonde look like a seven.

To Sydney, he looked like a regular sucker. She only needed $1,500 more before she had her goal for the trip. She came to Vegas about once a month to make enough money for rent, daycare, and all other expenses, allowing her to stay at home every day. She normally cleared about $10,000 easy because she hustled. She had the work ethic of a successful entrepreneur.

"My name is Sydney," she said before he could ask. She enjoyed leading conversation—she liked leading everything. She had been the captain of her high school cheer squad and the first woman in her family to graduate high school and go to college. She was a trailblazer and had just finished up a job in the alley minutes before she sat down next to Jacob.

"Are you here for business or pleasure?" he asked.

"Is there a difference?" She gave him a shy smile.

He smiled back. "Let's settle on both."

"Deal," she said. "I'm going to go freshen up in the little girls' room." She needed to get that alley guy's smell off her—this new guy seemed promising. "Will you order me a drink?"

"Sure!" he said. "It'll be here waiting for you when you get back."

"You're not going to ask what I want?"

"I know what you want."

She dug his confidence and wanted to know more about him. He reminded her of something or someone. She was a true beauty with an exotic look, the kind that never wanted for makeup. But when she put it on, it made her almost too beautiful to bear. She was five-four with the body of a gymnast: small on top and big on the bottom, just like he liked it.

Right off the bat, she was surprised by him—he seemed more mature than she'd assumed. He was nice, kind, and funny. "I'm gonna' fuck him for free," she thought and let out a huge laugh. Her thoughts drifted to Lamar, her former boyfriend and the reason she'd never been in a serious relationship. Lamar was her first love—she'd loved him more than anything—and this guy brought a lot of those dormant feelings back.

She had completely changed her life for Lamar. She started smoking, drinking, and skipping class. He would say everything would be fine, and she believed him. She lived and died on his every word. It was the first time anyone had ever shown her that kind of love. He was a pure soul, and although flawed, he gave her his heart completely. When she got pregnant, he asked her to marry him to prevent her from leaving. He wanted the kid to be named Lance after the famous cyclist who was going through adversity over doping. He would often tell her, "I get what that guy is going through. They did the same thing to me. There is so much pressure to be the best, and normal folks who aren't in this life don't get it."

Lamar died of a heart attack the day before Lance was born. The doctors were trying to revive him in the ER when Sydney went into labor. Lance was born, and she had to figure out how to support them. When she left the hospital, a few members from Lamar's family helped out periodically, but they were too busy blaming her for killing him.

She moved to California with the $8,000 Lamar left her. He had gotten it from a booster and said, "If anything ever happens to me, take this money and get outta here." It was enough for a deposit on a small place, and she figured she'd make up the rest somehow. That's when she met Dixie, a tall black girl from south Mississippi who would eventually become her best friend Dave.

On her way to the bathroom, she ran into the john from the alley. He grabbed her arm and wanted more. She took his number and told him she'd see him later, but only if he paid double. "You can have whatever you want, baby!" he said.

She had a way with guys; she knew it ever since she started having sex for money in junior high.

It all started because she wanted to get a bike for Christmas, but she was told that money didn't grow on trees. She decided to start selling lemonade on the street. Her uncle pulled up and said, "If you want some real money, come with me." She turned her first trick by accident because she literally thought it was a game. Because the guy was her uncle, he paid her to keep her mouth closed. "One hundred dollars," she thought. "That was easy!" He continued to pay her and taught her some tricks that she would eventually use as she got older.

When she returned to the bar, the handsome young man had ordered her a sidecar, a cocktail traditionally made with cognac, orange liqueur, and lemon juice. It was her favorite drink and the first thing Lamar ever bought for her.

How did he know? She grabbed it, drank it, and said, "Let's go!" She threw a $100 bill on the bar and said, "See you later, Dave!"

"A'ight sugar." Dave had known Sydney from the outset of her street career. He got out of the street-walking business due to illness and discovered that he wanted a dick. He was on phase 1 of the surgery.

Jacob was walking with her and sizing her up. He thought about the six-inch stilettoes, the red dress, the blondish purple hair, and the Louis Vuitton purse.

"Where's your room?" she asked

"Fourth floor. Where's yours?"

"Not here." She walked fast. He had to speed walk to keep up. As they started heading toward his room, she changed directions.

"Let's get a taxi. My room will be better."

They hopped in a taxi and were there in minutes. Always thinking about the next john, she wanted to be close to the money, and the money was in her hotel. But for a moment, she forgot about the money. As soon as they went in her room, it was magic for both of them. Jacob lost himself in her and immediately knew this was more than a one night stand. They kissed like they were in a new relationship. The passion between them was electric.

It had been almost an hour. Jacob looked up at her with amazement. He noticed that her skin was soft, but her eyes were hard. They looked like they had seen a lot. She smiled and said, "Be honest, are you married?"

He gave her a look that said, "Huh?" It was an odd question, but she was feeling something different with him, and she needed to get that out of the way.

"No, I'm not married. I do have a girlfriend. Her name is…"

"Good," she said, cutting him off. "I don't give a shit about her."

She ground back into him and kissed him deeply, with even more passion than before.

The room made the already incredible experience even better for Jacob. There were mirrors all over the place. Everywhere he looked, he could see her riding him. It was actually Dave's place. He had a deal with the hotel where he worked; he used to fuck the general manager when he was in the life.

Sydney always stayed at Dave's place, but Jacob was the first guy she'd ever brought there. Even Dave was surprised at the gesture, he later told her.

She climbed off him and brought him to the shower. She washed his body and started to give him boyfriend treatment—at least that's what his mind was telling him. He felt extremely comfortable, and they lay in bed talking until they fell asleep in each other's arms. They talked about life and why it mattered. They discussed world issues, wars, and why people judge. It was one of the best nights either of them had had.

The alarm went off, and they both jumped. He had to get on the road, and she had a plane to catch.

"Will I see you again?" she said. "I want to. I like you because you're honest and simple. Oh, and a good fuck!"

He laughed. "Likewise, baby. I could do this every day, but I need to take that from good to great."

"Me too."

They kissed and both had the sense that there were going to fall in love with each other. But for now, Sydney had to get home to little Junior, and Jacob needed to get back to Alyssa.

As she was about to leave the hotel, bags in tow, it hit her: "Shit. Lamar!"

She called all of her johns Lamar. She ran upstairs and knocked on the guy's door. He came to the door naked, and she walked right in. "Perfect!" She slammed the door and gave him the best four and a half minutes of his adult life. When it was over, she grabbed his wallet, pulled out all the money—$1,200—and told him she would see him next month. She left with a smile on her face. All in all, she had made $9,500 in one weekend, minus the $1,000 she gave Dave.

Easy money, she thought to herself. Too easy.

Lance

I t was the oh shit moment. She was sitting in the lounge chair of a swanky restaurant bathroom, praying she could face this guy with everything going on in her head. It was finally here, the moment she had been waiting on her entire life. The moment everyone dreams about, and like usual, she was on the cusp of pissing it away.

"Do I tell him or not? How will this play out? Is he really serious? Are we ready for this step? Do I keep it or not?" All these thoughts were running through her head. She was at dinner with Lance. He had just gotten a new job at some marketing company. She wasn't sure how any of this happened, but he was paying the bills. It had been months since she spent a dime, and she and Lance were having regular sex. But she had one major issue and didn't really know how to shake it. Lance had this black box in his jacket. He didn't think she noticed, but it fell out when they were getting dressed, and just as she was about to peek, he came out of the bathroom. She hurriedly slipped it back in his jacket.

She got excited and thought to herself about how many times she had wanted him to ask her to marry him. It was about to happen, but she was getting cold feet.

"Sydney, I need to ask you something."

"Yes, Lance?" she replied.

"Do you care about me?"

"Of course, honey!"

Just then, the waiter interrupted with water. "Really, dude?" Lance thought. "Do you not see what's happening here?"

Despite the interruption, it was one of the best moments of his life—she looked so incredible. "I've never noticed those earrings or that dress," he thought. "This is the most beautiful day of my life." He reached in his pocket, but his hand stayed hidden as he said, "Sydney, I really care about you—a lot. I want you and Junior to always be my family. I couldn't think of a better place to be right now, except right here with you. You have made my world better for being a part of it. I'm not myself when I'm around you. Will you…"

The food showed up, and he was once again interrupted.

"Excuse me, I really need to go tinkle," she said quickly.

Damnit, this was getting frustrating for him.

Now she was sitting in the bathroom trying to decide what to do about all the money, all the lies, all the wigs, all the Lamars. "How do I explain this shit?" she wondered aloud. Lance was such a good guy, but now she was sitting there feeling pregnant, thinking she needed to get rid of it. What about Jacob? Harris? Mort? Jimmy? Chi Wong? All of them would have to disappear, and she'd be exclusively with Lance. He wasn't boring, but oh shit—he was fixed! It finally hit her. Whose fucking baby was this?

At the table, the waitress caught Lance's eye. He was interested but wanted something else from her. He wanted some water, and she wanted some dick—at least that's what she asked for when she came by the table. "Excuse me, is this dick taken?" she said in a deep, raspy voice, making a hand gesture that would make any man blush.

Lance was taken aback. Just then, Sydney returned and gave the girl a look that said, "Make a move, bitch, and do it quickly!"

Even Lance was shocked by the look; she had never shown jealousy before, but it made him feel sexy to have them fight over him.

Sydney slid back into her seat, and he didn't even have to finish popping the question.

"Yes, of course I'll marry you, honey!" she said.

Lance felt like the happiest guy on the planet. All his plans were falling into place. He had a job and a family. He was looking at homes and pursuing other things. Their lives were changing for the better, and things were going according to his plan. Before they knew it, they were in the men's room.

"Give it to me," moaned Sydney.

He smiled and said, "Use your 'I'm having sex in the men's room and don't want to go to jail' voice."

But after that gentle scolding, he lost himself. He couldn't stop panting and having his way with her.

"Give it to me! Give it all to me!" she screamed.

"Uhhhhh!" he yelled as he unloaded into her.

They stayed like that for a moment, holding each other before they returned to reality.

_ "What a night! I'm getting fuckin' married?" she said out loud.

She had to decide what to do. She had always said that she would never, in a million years, have an abortion, but here she was, torn between being with a guy who really loved her or keeping the baby.

Ever since Lamar had passed, she thought of him every time she looked at Junior; she really enjoyed playing house with Lance, but she did not want Junior to have a brother or sister.

She was upset with herself for being so careless. It was so uncharacteristic, so out of the ordinary for her. She started going into her stash of cash frequently and taking fewer trips out of town.

When Lance finally met Dave, he didn't like him.

"What the hell is that?" he asked.

"He's my best friend in the whole world, and you will be nice to him. We have known each other for years. I love him like family."

Lance accepted Dave but didn't like the fact that a he was always hanging around. Lance was a bit homophobic and didn't really know how to feel about a transgender man who was born a woman.

For his part, Dave accepted Lance but warned Sydney: "You need to watch him. He has that itch."

"What itch?" she asked.

"The itch of an addict. He's on something, baby. I'm just not sure what it is yet. Just keep an eye on him and watch your stuff."

She said okay, but in her mind she thought Dave was being overprotective.

The next morning, Sydney woke up overjoyed, but her mind was still in a bad place. She had too many secrets to come clean about. She loved Lance, and she wanted to be his wife more than anything. There was no way she would mess this up. She knew the truth would hurt him, but if he loved her like she thought he did, there was nothing that would stop them from having their happily ever after. While Lance was at work, she thought about the best way to explain herself.

Sydney knew today would be tough, but it had to be done.

When Lance walked in the door from work, she'd already put the baby down and was waiting for him on the couch. She greeted him with a kiss and hugged him tight, as if it was the last time she'd be able to hold him like that. "Baby, have a seat," she said.

They both took a seat on the couch. Lance sat close to her, and she inched away a bit. She needed to put a little space between them just in case he got upset and she had to make her way to the nearest exit. Lance had never gotten physical with her before—he didn't seem like the type to put his hands on a woman. But she couldn't be sure. You never knew what a man might be provoked to do, especially with the type of information she was getting ready to drop. "Well," she thought, "Here goes."

"Baby, I am so happy you want to spend the rest of your life with me. This is a dream come true," she said with tears in her eyes.

"Don't cry, love," Lance said with all the care in the world in his voice but a look of confusion on his face.

Sydney looked him in the eyes and said, "I have something to tell you. You know how I've been going to Vegas to help my grandmother when she gets sick? Well…"

Lance interrupted her. "Sydney, if you're trying to come clean about running back and forth between here and Vegas, sleeping with all those niggas for money, I know all about it."

Sydney's mouth hung open in total shock. She couldn't believe he knew her secrets.

"I found the money months ago in Junior's diaper bags," he said. "I was surprised at how much money you had in the house. I knew your job was good," Lance said, "but I knew it wasn't paying that damn good. I did some research of my own. Your granny does live in Vegas. She ain't sick, though. Then it hit me—going to Vegas every other weekend to care for your sick grandmother, and then you have all this cash hidden in the house. I'm nobody's fool, Sydney.

"This is why I asked you to marry me. You dance, right? I want you out of the game. The fact that you even felt you had to live like that says I wasn't doing my job. I'm your man; you are my queen. You are of out of the game, and I'll do what I have to do to provide for this house and this family."

Sydney smiled at Lance. That was all she needed to hear. She told the whole story from beginning to end. She told him about Lamar and everyone who had been between them since he died.

Five months later, they were standing outside the house they had bought with the money they saved together.

Sydney had always wanted an intimate ceremony. Everyone she knew was there, and all of Lance's co-workers were in attendance. He made a dedication to his sister, and she made a dedication to family. The wedding party wore pink and gray, with the guys in gray suits and pink ties while the girls wore pink gowns. The wedding was set outdoors in a park they both loved. The aisle was lined with lights and rose petals. They didn't have the traditional setup of a bride and groom's side. They wanted everyone to be seated in the middle. Both Lance and Sydney were welcoming—no division to their wedding. They wanted everyone to feel as one.

On their wedding invites, they noted, "Everyone is welcome to the wedding; not the marriage." They didn't want to be caught up with other people's view of how their marriage should go. They did, however, welcome advice from those married couples they admired, including Lance's parents. Junior served as the ring bearer. He had barely started walking and was the cutest thing you ever saw. He looked like a teddy bear from Build-a-Bear walking down the aisle with his little suit on. When they looked out at the guests, their hearts smiled. They asked the guests to wear white, as they wanted to preserve the fact that Lance's sister was unable to attend but always wanted a white wedding.

They were married and living a happy life. Well, almost happy. Dave was no longer in the picture because he was locked up. It was the only thing that made Sydney sad on her wedding day. After the reception was over, she sat down and penned a long letter to Dave, who was in San Quentin serving time for money laundering and embezzlement. They wanted to stick Marcus's murder on him, too, but no one could put the gun in his hand.

Candis

Candis was in the shower getting ready for work when she heard her phone ringing. "Damn," she said out loud. The ringtone told her it was Campbell. She'd normally ignore phone calls while she was in the shower, but Campbell was an exception to that rule. She reached for her towel, wrapped herself in it, and proceeded to the bedroom, where her phone was on the charger.

"Hey baby, what's happening?" He always greeted her that way, and although it had been years since she first heard it, she still loved it. "Look, I don't really know how else to say this, but I need you to clear your schedule out for next week because we have a trip planned."

"Wait, what?" asked Candis.

"You heard me young lady!" he said, this time with a smile in his voice. "This is a special trip. I need this to happen next week."

"What's so special about next week?" Candis wondered.

Campbell pressed. "Babe."

"Okay, okay. I'm good for next week."

"Good. Love you. Gotta run back to this meeting."

He was so excited to tell her about the surprise he had planned for them, but he needed it to build for another week.

Candis's mind went wild. What could possibly be so great about next week? Where were they going this time? He did want to go to Niagara Falls, but he wanted to do that trip with his kid. Her mind would race all week.

But just a couple days later, he couldn't help himself anymore and told her—they were going to Brazil! He knew she'd always wanted to go there. That heads-up gave her a little time to shop, too.

Candis couldn't contain herself as she strolled through the hottest fashions at Saks. It wasn't that she was new to fancy clothes and designer labels. No, she was true to that. She was just so excited for the trip. She wanted to buy one of everything, but she tried to hold back. But for sure, she was thinking at least two new bathing suits for her and a couple shirts and shorts for him.

Just thinking about being on a trip with him—her chocolaty Adonis—in such a tropical place made her want to cream her panties right there in the shoe department. She had to hold it together. She only wanted to cum when she was with him, and surely, she could wait two days. While browsing through the shoes, a pair of Christian Louboutins caught her eye. The handcrafted, beaded shoes were perfect for a trip to Brazil! She couldn't wait until he saw her in these.

"Yes, I'll take them!" she thought as she headed to the sales clerk to ask for her size to try on. The clerk was a younger girl, maybe in her twenties. Her eyes were dark brown and pure, and she had a smile that could light up a room. She reminded Candis of herself. She looked as though she had a story to tell, but she masked it well. Candis approached her, read her nametag, and smiled. "Excuse me, Erin. Do you have these in a size eight?"

Erin smiled back and said, "Ma'am, let me go check for you."

"Ma'am?" Candis said. "Please don't call me that. It makes me feel old."

"I'm sorry," Erin said as she headed to the back to retrieve the shoes. She came back from the stock room holding the shoes in her hand as if they were trophies. She handed the shoes to Candis, who tried them on and strutted to the mirror to see how they looked. Indeed, they were perfect. They looked even better on her feet. Candis knew the shoes looked great, but she wanted Erin's opinion.

"Erin, how do you think these look?"

"Those shoes are fye!"

Candis giggled. She had heard some of the kids she volunteered with use the term "fye." When she was growing up, the word was "tight." Candis handed the shoes back to Erin, who boxed them, rang them up, and bagged them. Candis pulled out her credit card and paid for the shoes. Then she slid her hand in her purse and pulled out a $100 bill. The bill was folded so small it fit in the palm of her hand. She took the bag from Erin and slid the bill in her hand, just like her grandmother would do when she was a teenager. Erin looked down in her hand and told Candis she couldn't accept it, that it was against company policy to accept tips.

"It will keep you honest," Candis said, insisting that she take it.

Erin smiled and nodded a thank you. Candis wasn't sure what it was, but she saw a lot of herself in that girl. Almost too much. Candis continued shopping in Saks, running her credit card bill up. When she was satisfied with the items she'd gotten herself and her man, she headed home to pack.

The next morning, Candis sent him a text that read: "One more day!"

He didn't respond, but she didn't care. She was on too much of a high to be bothered.

Candis continued throwing last-minute things into her suitcase and mentally preparing herself for the long flight the next day. She was going to bed early tonight. Her clothes were already laid on the bed in the guest room. When she traveled, she loved to be cute and comfortable. She had settled on a pair of printed leopard leggings from J.Crew, a basic black Gap T-shirt, and a pair of Cole Haan drivers. "Perfect," she thought. "He won't be able to resist my ass in these leggings." Candis went to sleep and dreamed about waking up on the perfect vacation with him.

When she woke up the next morning, she rushed to the airport. She didn't want to take any chances on missing her flight. She parked her car in Lot A, the closest lot to the departure terminals. It cost more, but she didn't mind. All she had to do was drop her bag off at the check-in counter. She'd had already checked in online—she did that the very minute she could. She breezed through airport security without a hitch and then had enough time left to post up at Starbucks and people watch. You could count on some characters walking through LAX. Obviously, the airport was where the weirdoes came every two minutes. Candis couldn't control her smile or laughter from all the foolishness. She laughed so much and smiled so hard that you would have thought she was watching an episode of BET's *Comic View*.

When she finished her coffee, high on life, she proceeded to gate C-28. She double checked the screen: "Flight 0892: Departure time: 10:30, Rio de Janeiro."

"Yep that's it," she said to herself. She was right on time. The flight would start boarding business class any minute. She walked on the plane and took her seat up front by the window. Since she was a child, she loved having the window seat. She would imagine herself sitting on the soft clouds, catching rainbows. Before the cabin crew even finished going over the inflight announcements and safety demonstrations, she was already sleeping like a baby, dreaming of all the things she planned to do to and with him on their trip. She finally stopped dozing about halfway through the fourteen-and-a-half-hour flight to use the restroom and stretch her legs. She had worn compression socks to keep her blood circulating and her feet from swelling on the lengthy flight. When she returned to her seat, there was a meal waiting on her tray table. Everything was just working out perfectly. She loved eating the meals they served on international flights. It was always delicious, and this meal was especially good.

She couldn't help but wondering, though, if she was just loving everything at the moment. She checked out her seatmate, an older white gentleman who reminded her a bit of former president George Bush, and he was scarfing his meal down in record time. "Damn," she thought. "It must be that good."

The airline offered free Wi-Fi, and she thought it would be a good time to pull out her laptop and check to see if she had an e-mail from Campbell. She booted up her MacBook Air and went to the Gmail account she'd set up specifically for their communication. Sure enough, as soon as she logged in, she saw a new message from CLovesC@gmail.com:

> *Hey Sweetheart,*
> *My flight has been delayed. When you get to the airport, you don't have to wait on my flight to land like we originally planned. I will meet you at the hotel. They will have keys waiting for you at the front desk.*
>
> *Love you,*
> *C.*

Candis immediately got upset—so upset that she wanted to cry, but she didn't want the other passengers to know she was having a breakdown. She decided to take some Advil PM and try to go back to sleep for the remainder of the flight. It worked. Candis woke up as the plane was landing. She grabbed her carry-on from the overhead bin and walked slowly to customs. Other passengers were rushing by her, probably wondering why she was moving so slowly. She didn't care. She didn't have a reason to rush. Her man's flight was delayed. When she finally made it through customs, she went through more security and headed to baggage claim. She was in such a mood that she was walking with her head down. She didn't notice Campbell already at the baggage claim area holding a dozen pink roses in his hand, with a smile so bright it could shame the whitest snowfall on the first day of winter.

When she finally looked up and saw him standing there, she couldn't help but smile. Here she was walking around the airport in Brazil with her stank attitude thinking his flight was delayed and she wouldn't see him until later, and here he was, there early to surprise her.

The trip already offered a wonderful surprise, and it had only just begun. They exited Galeao International Airport hand in hand and walked to the waiting car Campbell had arranged. He took Candis's hand, opened her door, and watched her slide into the backseat.

"Look at that ass," he thought. She knew he loved to see her in a nice pair of leggings. The way they gripped her butt, she might as well not have anything on. He couldn't wait to get her to the room. The driver pulled up to the Grand Hyatt Rio de Janeiro in no time. Campbell got out of the back first and didn't even let the driver get Candis's door. When she was with him, she didn't need any other man, and he made that very clear. Candis loved that about him. He always took care of her and tended to her needs.

They walked in the lobby and approached the concierge counter to check in. They got in line behind a young couple and their baby. Immediately, sadness washed over Candis. "Why isn't this my life?" she thought. "Why am I not checking into a hotel on vacation with my new baby?" Tears filled her eyes. She reached into her purse, grabbed a Kleenex, and started to dab at her eyes.

"Sweetheart, is everything all right?" Campbell asked.

She smiled through her tears and said weakly, "It must be all of these beautiful flowers that have my allergies acting up."

After they checked in and had the bellhop take their bags to the room, they set out to explore. Of course, Candis wanted to go to the mall, and Campbell wanted to find the closest beach. He didn't take many days off, though, so Candis set her shopping urge aside so he could have a day full of relaxation. Since their hotel had a private beach, they decided to head back to the room so they could change into their swimsuits.

Campbell was ready first. He wore a pair of red and white swim trunks that Candis didn't really care for. "Where in the world did you get those?" she asked.

"Ashley bought these for me when we went to Jamaica," he replied without thinking.

As soon as he said it, he knew he should have thought of some lie.

Candis laughed. "She must have gotten those cheap-ass looking trunks from Walmart?"

He laughed, too, because Ashley did in fact get them from Walmart. Ashley wasn't into fashion and designers like Candis. She was simple and mostly did last-minute shopping. Candis reached into her bag and pulled out her Louis Vuitton navy and white bathing suit. It was a one-shoulder ruffled swimsuit with a gold zipper down the side. She tossed Campbell a pair of navy and white Dolce and Gabana trunks she'd picked out at Saks.

"Wear these instead," she said. She thought they matched perfectly with her swimsuit.

They enjoyed the pool, stopping to orders drinks, flirting, and kissing like two high school kids in love. Their love was genuine and often misunderstood by Candis's friends. They finished each other's sentences and always knew what the other was thinking. It was good for the two of them. After a few hours of lounging around and enjoying everything that was going on around them, they decided to get out of the sun and head to the room. Candis went to sit on the bed and turned on the TV to see what else the hotel had to offer. Campbell went to the bathroom, removed his swim trunks, and started the shower. When Candis heard the water running, that was her cue. Whenever they were together, they showered together.

Candis opened the shower door. "Can I join you?" she said, looking him in the eyes so as not to be distracted by his penis. If she looked down, she would want to take him in her mouth, and that would start a fuck fest in there. She wasn't in the mood to have shower sex. She wanted him in the bed.

"Of course, baby," he said. "You always know the answer to that."

She got in facing Campbell while he stood with his back to the cascading water. She shrieked when it hit her. "This water is cold!" she exclaimed.

Per usual, Campbell had the water set to lukewarm. Candis never understood how men could take lukewarm showers. She, like the other women she knew, liked the shower piping hot.

"I knew you'd want to burn the skin off me," he said with a laugh. "One second, babe, and you can come up here." He turned to face the shower head to continue washing himself. Candis picked up one of the face towels and started to get it sudsy with bubbles so she could wash his back. She loved doing that while leaning in to kiss his neck every now and again. He loved it, too.

They switched positions so he could wash her back, and Candis turned up the heat. Campbell got out of the shower while she finished and headed to the room to set the mood.

"Great!" Candis thought. "I can turn this water up some more." She got out of the shower after finishing up, wrapped herself in the hotel robe, then pranced into the room so Campbell would notice her.

"You don't gotta do all that, baby. I see you when you're coming."

She smiled and kept on prancing to the bed. Campbell came to her and slowly took off her robe, admiring her beautiful figure. "Damn baby, you so fine."

"Thanks love. I try."

"Lie down so I can rub you down and give you what you've been missing."

"How you know I've been missing it?" she said with a giggle.

"Because don't nobody do you like Big C!" he said.

"You're right about that, baby," Candis said as she lay down with her breasts up and her nipples pointing to the ceiling. He grabbed some essential oils from his bag. When it came to Candis, he went all out. He wanted her to have and experience the best. She deserved it. She had always seemed to play second fiddle to her sister—it was something he noticed right when he and Ashley started dating. He thought he loved Candis then but couldn't be sure. That uncertainty started to fade right away, though, and now, in their room in Brazil, he had peppermint oil, lavender oil, sandalwood, and jasmine. Jasmine was Candis's favorite. He took a little of each oil in his palms, creating the perfect aroma to mix with the candles he'd already lit.

"A massage by candlelight," Candis said, smiling. "It must be my lucky day."

"Girl, you just don't know how lucky you're about to get!"

He began slowly massaging her feet, working his way up to her inner thighs. Candis had her eyes closed. She started moaning as soon as his oiled hands began to knead themselves up her body. It felt incredible. He took his thumbs and applied pressure to each thigh as he worked his magical hands over every part of her lower body. He continued working his way up. The next stop was the twins. He took each of her swollen breasts in his palms, slowly taking her nipples in between his thumb and forefinger and pinching and rubbing them slightly.

"Oooh, baby," Candis moaned. "Stop or you're gonna make me cum."

"Not yet love."

He smiled and kissed each nipple before telling Candis to turn over. Of course, she did as she was told. She enjoyed this; she loved being next to him, loved him caressing her. She wanted this moment to last forever. Campbell massaged her back better than any masseuse ever had. He was the truth. He worked her aching back—she hadn't even realized it was sore—then turned her over and started to kiss her passionately. Candis was a very impatient lover when it came to Campbell. She wanted him to be inside her now, but she knew she had to slow and cherish these moments when he could take his time and not have to rush back to Ashley's side. It didn't help that he teased her—kissing her neck, massaging her nipples, rubbing his hard shaft against her opening.

Campbell was just about to enter her when Candis couldn't take it any longer. She grabbed him and put him at her entrance. He smiled—he'd tortured her long enough.

He entered her slowly. He knew it had been a while, and she was tight. Every time they made love, it felt like the first time. He loved the way her pussy muscles grasped his dick. It was the best feeling ever, like she'd been created just for him. He was always told that women who had total control over their pussy muscles were dangerous. With Candis's looks, style, professional demeanor, great sex, and bomb-ass head, she was a force to be reckoned with. If he didn't hurry up and put a ring on her finger, someone else would snatch her up for sure.

He looked Candis in her eyes while they moved together, both trying to make sure the other was enjoying every moment. He smiled at her. He loved this woman. He had known being with Ashley was a mistake from the first time he laid eyes on Candis, and he was about to right all his wrongs. All he needed was for Candis to say yes and Ashley to sign the papers. He could feel Candis about to orgasm beneath him. Her legs shook uncontrollably when she was about to cum.

"Hold on, baby. Don't cum yet. Cum with Daddy," Campbell whispered, nibbling on her ear.

Candis started to fuck Campbell back, moving her hips violently and squeezing her pussy tighter on his dick. She needed him to get to where she was. She was about to cum, and she didn't consider herself to be a selfish lover. She could feel Campbell's penis start to fill as his pumps grew faster and more intense. They were about to cross the threshold of ecstasy together.

"I'm about to cum!" she said.

"I'm cumming with you!" Campbell exclaimed, thrusting into Candis one last time before releasing himself inside her.

Campbell rolled to his side, sweaty and out of breath. "Baby, I love you, and I love what you do to me."

She looked at him. "I love you back, babe." She just wished he was hers forever. She was getting tired of sharing him—with her sister, no less. At least she could have him in her dreams as they both drifted off to sleep.

The next morning, Campbell woke Candis up like he always did, with his head buried between her legs, blessing her yoni like only he could. Candis loved the way he made his tongue dance on her clit. She looked down at him between her legs.

"Good morning, babe," she whimpered.

He took a break between the soft kisses and suckling on her sweetness to say, "Good morning, baby." He always said Candis was his breakfast in bed. She didn't mind being on the menu one bit.

After their morning rendezvous, Campbell and Candis showered together. Campbell was dressed and ready to go before Candis, so he sat on the bed listening to music as she finished getting ready. "We've got somewhere to be at a certain time, C," Campbell said.

Candis could hear his patience growing thin with her. She hated to be rushed, but for him, she could speed up the process. She was ready to go in five. "See, I'm ready, babe, in record time." Candis smiled and softly kissed his lips. He extended his arm for her to hold it as they headed out of the room to the hotel lobby, where the same driver from yesterday was waiting with the car door already open for Candis to climb in. Candis slid in the backseat, and Campbell followed.

"Where are we going?" Candis asked.

"It's a surprise, love. Just sit back and relax."

She couldn't imagine what kind of surprise Campbell had planned for her now. She was nervous and excited at the same time. They rode through downtown Rio, or "Centro," as the locals called it. It was full of historical landmarks and housed several cathedrals and museums.

"Isn't it beautiful?" Campbell asked.

"It's amazing!" She was like a kid in a candy store. After taking in the scenery for about twenty minutes, they pulled up to a beautiful villa that was several stories tall and protected by a security gate.

"Who lives here?" Candis asked, puzzled. She didn't think Campbell knew anyone in Rio or that he had any clients near here.

Campbell smiled and reached for her hand. "We live here...if you love it."

Candis was taken aback for a moment. *The house was theirs?* He couldn't have said that. "How?"

"Baby, I love you. This is why I wanted to take this trip now. This is the surprise I've been planning for you, for us. I know it has taken some time for me to get everything in order, but I meant what I said about leaving her. I know this will not be easy, but together we can make it work. As God as my witness, I love you more than life itself."

Candis smiled and looked up at Campbell. "Baby, I love you so much. You don't understand how happy this makes me."

Her mind was racing. She wanted to melt. She couldn't believe it was finally happening for her. "Finally, someone loves me for me," she thought. "I am good enough, and I do matter." Candis was filled with an excitement that she had never felt, thinking about how much she loved this man. Everyone said he wouldn't leave his wife, even Linda. "They all doubted me," thought Candis. "Now we are not only in love, but we have a place in another country. We *will raise our kids* in another country." Candis ran to the front door and opened it. The floor in the foyer was white marble. There was a staircase to her right. She rushed up that staircase with pride. This was her house, and she walked the stairs like she owned it—because she did. There were four floors, four bedrooms, seven bathrooms, and three balconies.

Candis, of course, wanted to see the master suite. She turned on her heels, and Campbell was right behind her. "Where's our room?" she asked.

"I thought you'd never ask." He guided her to a room on the third floor—the master suite. It was breathtaking. It had hardwood floors, his and hers closets, a huge bathroom with heated marble floors. Candis had seen heated marble floors on an episode on HGTV. She thought one day they'd be in her house, but she didn't think it would happen this soon.

The shower was big enough for ten people to fit inside. There was a rain shower, as well as jets coming from the wall at every angle. She walked back out into the fully furnished bedroom. Campbell had done an amazing job. If she didn't know him so well , she would assume he'd hired an interior decorator.

"Baby, I wanted to decorate this room for us," he said. "If there's anything you don't like or want to change, please let me know. I wanted this room to be done tonight so we could stay here this evening. I have one more surprise for you, though."

He looked Candis in the eyes and grabbed her hands.

What else could he possibly have up his sleeve? She was already about to pass out from the excitement. "Turn around, baby. Walk out on the balcony."

Candis did as she was told and opened the French doors to the balcony. She walked to the railing and looked down, taking in the beautiful view. The water was amazingly blue, the hillside was full of trees, and the skies couldn't have been brighter. She was searching the atmosphere for whatever it was Campbell wanted her to see. She couldn't find it.

"What am I looking for?" she asked, turning back around to face him.

"This," he said.

Candis's mouth fell open. Campbell was on one knee, holding the most exquisite diamond ring she'd ever seen: a rose gold, cushion-cut diamond with more diamonds lining the band. In her most elaborate fantasies, she didn't see rings like this. It had to be at least three carats. Tears started to stream down Candis's face; first cute tears, and then she started bawling. She tried to cover her face, but he wouldn't let her hands go.

He started to speak, but he was all choked up, too. He closed his eyes for a second to steel himself. Then he opened them and said, "Candis, will you marry me? This is our home. We will live here and raise our wonderful children and have a wonderful life together." Campbell smiled and watched for her reaction. He knew this was a lot for her to take in after everything he'd done to her.

Through her sobbing, Candis answered with a barely coherent, "Yes."

"What was that, love?"

When Candis's sobs were under control, she repeated herself. "Yes."

Overcome with emotion, Candis fainted on the balcony, banging her head against the railing. She had to be rushed to the hospital, where she was put into a medication-induced coma.

Campbell knew he couldn't contact Ashley because he wouldn't be able to explain why he was with her sister out of the country. He spoke with the doctor, who assured him Candis was stable enough to be transported back to the States for proper treatment.

It was a long flight back home. This gave Campbell time to gather his thoughts about how to break the news to Ashley. He prayed like hell that Candis was all right. He blamed himself for everything that was happening and shed a tear at the thought of losing the love of his life. Why had he been such a coward, he thought as he sat silently on the plane.

When he arrived in California, Campbell called Candis's father and explained what had happened in Brazil. He tried to explain why Candis was there. Her father had a lot of questions and quickly put it together that Candis and Campbell had gone to Brazil together.

"My God, son, how could you? I mean, they are sisters, for crying out loud. Was there not enough out there? You might rot in hell for this one. But I know you didn't have to call me, and I'm happy you called. I'll help my daughters the best way I can, but you are going to have to own this one, young man. You need to call Ashley and explain everything. She does not need to be shocked when she gets to the hospital."

"Yes, sir," Campbell said wearily.

From there, everything unraveled—all the secrets, all the lies. They'd tried so hard to hide their deceit, but now here it was, laid bare.

Justin

The investigator called Justin and asked if he would meet him at the station. He had Dave in custody.

"I'm near the station," Justin said. "I'll be there in a few minutes."

They had Dave in custody, but he'd had no time to contact his lawyer. When he killed Pete, an undercover ATF agent was in the room. He radioed in the homicide, and the police picked up Dave when he arrived home. The investigator just needed Justin to corroborate Dave's whereabouts on the day Marcus was killed.

Justin walked in the door and was immediately filled with rage. "Let me at him," he hissed, attempting to burst through the door to where they were holding Dave. "He killed Marcus!"

The investigator and other members of the unit grabbed Justin. "Hold on, son. Let's get him the right way." They were able to calm him down.

Dave would eventually get more than ten years for murder. Sydney didn't have to snitch; Dave confessed to the murder and kept Bianca and Sydney out of trouble. He also kept his business in tact and continued to run things remotely from prison.

Justin came to terms with the fact that Marcus's actual killer was never going to be captured, but he took heart in the fact that the person responsible for his death was behind bars. Justin would go on to graduate from college and become an officer in the military. He dedicated his entire career to the memory of Marcus, naming his first son after his beloved friend.

Ashley

While running through the house getting ready for work on Monday morning, Ashley couldn't find her leather portfolio. She had a big presentation at work, and she needed that portfolio—it was a good-luck charm. She couldn't remember where she'd had it last or if she'd left it at work. She needed something to put her handouts and notes in, though, and she wasn't leaving unprepared. Campbell always had that kind of stuff just lying around his office, so she went in to see what she could find.

And right there on his desk, a brown leather portfolio. "This will do," she thought. "Let me just take out these papers, and I can put my stuff inside." When Ashley opened the portfolio, she couldn't believe her eyes. She almost wished she hadn't found it. "How could he be so careless to leave something like this lying around?" she thought. She didn't understand what was going on, but she was going to get to the bottom of it one way or another.

The type of relationship she thought she had with her husband was one in which she would just call him and ask what she wanted to know. This time was different. She knew he wouldn't be straightforward. She was furious, but that fury quickly became tears. She preferred the fury. Crying *was not* Ashley's thing. She didn't consider herself an overly emotional woman. Hell, she'd been through so much that a lot of things didn't even faze her anymore. But this pierced her heart.

She was at a loss for words. All she could think was: "How could he do this to me?" He was supposed to be her Prince Charming forever. Ashley knew there had been some infidelity through the years, but never in a million years did she think they would be headed for a divorce.

"Ha!" she said aloud. Who was she fooling? She had known the type of man Campbell was when she met him. She had simply decided to look past it. Her father's words came back to her: "A tiger doesn't change its stripes." She knew that, but it still hurt because she thought she was different—an exception to the rule.

Ashley decided to call into work. She got her assistant on the phone. "Hello Nicole. This is Ashley. I won't be coming into the office today. I had an emergency come up. Reschedule my meeting for tomorrow. Oh, and Nicole, please forward all calls to my cell. Thanks."

Ashley hung up, pleased that she'd done a good enough job masking the turmoil. Then she called Candis, but her sister's phone went straight to voicemail. "That's strange," Ashley thought. "We usually talk every morning."

She wasn't going to take this lying down. Ashley picked up her phone one more time. "Hello. This is Ashley Jones. I'd like to speak to Attorney Brinks. Yes, I'll hold."

By the time she'd scheduled a late-morning meeting with Johnathan Brinks from Brinks and Associates, it was already nine o' clock. She went to take off her work clothes and throw on something more casual for the meeting. She grabbed the papers from Campbell's desk as she left the house, then called her sister one more time. Still no answer. She really needed someone to talk to, and Candis was the only person she felt comfortable talking to about what was going on.

"Why is this heifer not answering her phone?" Ashley said as she got in the car. She decided that she would just drive over to Candis's place. She pulled up to her sister's house and parked in the driveway. It was weird that Candis's car wasn't there. She usually went into work a little later. "She must have parked in the garage," Ashley thought. She reached in her purse and pulled out the key Candis had given her for emergencies. "Hell, if this ain't an emergency, I dunno what is," Ashley thought.

She opened the door. "Candis!" she yelled through the house. "Candis, wake yo' ass up!"

There was no response. She went to the garage to see if Candis's car was there—nope. "Where could she be?" Ashley wondered. She never left the house this early. She knew where to look. Candis kept an iPad next to her bed, and she'd told Ashley that if she ever couldn't find her, to check the iPad—the location on her phone was always on. Ashley ran upstairs to retrieve it. She turned it on. Candis was close by, and it looked like she was at the hospital.

"The hospital? Why the hell would Candis be in the hospital? Please God, don't let it be something horrible," she thought but quickly dismissed it.

Her phone buzzed. It was Campbell, but she had no time for his lies, and it only pissed her off seeing as how she had the divorce papers in the car. "The nerve of this motherfucker," she said aloud.

She turned off Candis's iPad and left her house. As she pulled out of the driveway, she made a mental note to try Candis again later. Was that her diary by the bed? Her mind was going crazy as she drove to her meeting. When she got to a red light, she pulled the divorce papers out again. She saw the date. They'd been prepared only last week. Questions raced through her mind.

"How long has he been planning this? How long has my marriage been over? What am I going to do?" Tears rolled down her cheeks, but Ashley didn't even notice she was crying—she was so numb. She was in such a daze she didn't realize the light had turned green. *Beep! Beeeeeeep!* Cars honked at her. She wiped her tears and apologized by throwing her hand up in the rearview mirror.

She pulled up to the offices of Jonathan Brinks and Associates. She didn't know him, but she'd heard good things about his representation. She wiped her eyes, reapplied her mascara, and checked her makeup. She was not walking in looking like she'd already lost this thing. She always had to keep it cute, no matter what. She remembered what her pastor said: "During tough times, you have to look like what you're going to, not what you're going through."

Ashley got out of the car and marched into the law firm like a woman on a mission.

The secretary, an older white lady with silver hair and a pleasant smile, checked Ashley in. Ashley took a breath and gathered herself. She still couldn't believe this was happening.

"Ashley?" a voice boomed from the back of the office. She looked up and saw Melvin, her ex from high school. His parents were military, and they had moved away after her junior prom. He was the first person she loved—she also lost her virginity to him. She immediately felt safe when she looked at him. She jumped out of her seat and gave him the biggest hug.

"Jonathan is caught up," he said. "I'll help you, what's going on? How are Candis and your parents? It's really good to see you. I didn't know you lived here."

"Oh my God, Melvin, it's so much," Ashley burst out. "I found divorce papers this morning." She started to tear up. Melvin quickly grabbed her by the hand and led her to his office. He didn't want anyone to see her have a breakdown in the lobby.

Once they got inside his office, he took Ashley's jacket and hung it on the coat rack. He told her to have a seat. "Would you like something to drink? Water, tea?"

Ashley declined. She opened her mouth to begin telling him about what she'd found this morning, but she started to sob uncontrollably.

"It's okay, take your time. I understand. I just went through a divorce myself," Melvin said gently.

Ashley finished wiping her tears. "I'm sorry. I don't know where those emotions came from. Sorry to hear about your divorce as well."

"Oh, it's no big deal anymore. Sometimes you think you've found the one, and they turn out to be nothing like you expected. It happens to the best of us. Enough about me. What can I help you with today?"

"Today I found some divorce papers in my husband's office. It seems that the paperwork was just completed last week." Ashley handed the papers to Melvin.

He scanned them then fixed his gaze back on her.

"Did you know this was about to happen?" he asked. "Was there any inkling of this? What's your marriage been like?"

She really had thought everything was fine. In her own selfish way, she couldn't imagine anyone leaving her. Campbell had threatened it several times, but nothing really came of it. He had found out about the lavish spending on Rodeo Drive, the hidden credit cards, and all the money she was sending home to keep her family afloat. Not that it bothered Campbell that she sent money back home; what bothered him was that she sent obscenely large amounts of money home.

"Damn," Ashley thought. "I hope I didn't drive him to do this because I didn't take his threats seriously."

"Well?" Marvin said, looking into Ashley's eyes.

"Uh, no…" she said. "I mean, he has threatened divorce in the past, but I've always brushed it off. Besides, recently everything has been good between us."

"I know this is a hard question, but what did you come in seeking today? What is it that you want to walk away with?"

"I don't know. It's true that he makes more than I do, but I'm no stranger to hard work. I really want to keep the lifestyle for me and my son, and I don't want him to suffer because of some poor decisions two adults made. He deserves better than that. I can make my own money. I just can't believe this is happening to me." Ashley put her hands over her face and began to cry again.

Melvin walked around his desk and gave her a familiar hug. He was warm, just as she remembered. She couldn't believe she had been so stupid and didn't see this coming. She was overcome with emotion. It was embarrassing and hurtful, but there was also a sense of relief. She was less upset about the divorce and more upset about the fact that her life was changing. She'd always had a special place in her heart for Melvin. The hug brought back major emotions.

"Thank you, Melvin," she said. "I really did miss you. I'm just sorry we're catching up under these circumstances."

He smiled and said, "Never mind all that. Let's get you together. I'll walk you downstairs."

Melvin stopped at his secretary's desk and told her to hold his appointments for the rest of the afternoon. Then he paused and asked, "Have you eaten, Ashley?"

"No, not yet."

"Janice," he said to his secretary, "please make us a reservation at that restaurant I always go to with my high-maintenance clients." He glanced at Ashley with a smile. She looked up, realizing he was being playful.

Over lunch, they caught up on years of life and gossip. After about an hour, it felt like there was no longer any space between them. "Look, if you're ready to get out," Melvin said, "we can make a clean break. Why be with someone who doesn't want to be with you? That's not the typical advice I give to my clients, but this is it. Let them be, and we can start anew."

Ashley paused, looking back in her mind at the lies and realizing that the bad times outweighed the good. "Okay, Melvin. I'll give him what he wants," she said. "I'm exhausted."

Ashley was at Melvin's office when she got the call from her dad that Candis had arrived at the hospital. She rushed over. She was really nervous; on the one hand, she felt bad that she was in the hospital in such a condition. On the other hand, she was dealing with her own issues, and once again, she needed to put her feelings aside to take care of someone else. She was tired of being walked over and having to be strong for everyone; she wanted someone to be strong for her.

When she arrived at the hospital, she went to Candis's room and sat at her bedside, watching and waiting for any change. She sat there for hours; even when her father left, she stayed looking after her sister. A nurse came by to check on Candis. Ashley told her everything was fine and that she'd be leaving shortly to get some rest. She had already decided that she'd stay at Candis's house that night. Cooper was at a friend's house, and she just couldn't face Campbell. She knew he would most likely be back from his business trip that evening.

Candis lived close to the hospital, and Ashley wanted to make sure she could reach her sister quickly if anything changed. On her way out, she left her number at the nurse's station.

Ashley made it to Candis's house in record time. She was so incredibly tired. She fell asleep in the chair—she had been going so hard all day that she forgot to eat. After sleeping for a couple of hours, she got up to take a shower. She hadn't packed any clothes, so she went to Candis's dresser to grab some pajamas, then headed into the bathroom. She loved Candis's shower; it had multiple shower heads, just like at a spa. This gave her a few moments of relief in what was otherwise a crazy day.

Her phone continued to buzz. She had fourteen missed calls from Campbell. She finally decided to call him back after her shower. She jumped out and looked at herself in the mirror. She had so many questions: Was she still pretty enough? Sexy? She thought she had lost all the baby weight. Why did he want a divorce? Why did he want to break up their family? She started to cry but stopped herself, saying firmly, "Girl, it's not your fault."

She left the bathroom and took a seat on the chair in the bedroom. She picked up her phone to check social media, needing a distraction from the day's insanity. She read a few posts and watched a few videos, but nothing really pulled her out of her rut. She decided to turn on the news, but like social media, it didn't hold her attention. She looked down at her nails and decided she need to clip them. She riffled through Candis's drawer, searching for the clippers, and spotted what looked like Candis's journal. She opened to page one, and what she read floored her:

> *Today I started sleeping with my sister's husband, and I have decided that I love him and I want him to leave her for good.*

She read futher:

> *Today I called my man, and he was once again unavailable. I hate that he is with that bitch and that it makes me feel like shit. Am I not worthy of his time? His attention? His affection? He doesn't even know about the first abortion. It belonged to him, and he doesn't know how hard it was for me to have a second abortion. I question whether he loves me like I love him.*

Ashley couldn't believe it. She started breathing hard, Her eyes had to be playing tricks on her. There was no way Candis had been sleeping with Campbell. "Is this

153

why he wants a divorce?" she wondered out loud. She went from feeling numb to feeling angry.

"That little bitch," said Ashley through clenched teeth. She was pissed. She dropped the diary on the floor and just stood in place for several minutes. She remembered all the birthday parties, the sacrifices she'd made for her sister over the years. She wanted to kill her sister, but she was already in the hospital dying.

She got up and drove to the hospital. She wanted answers. She *needed* answers. She called her dad crying; he knew what was wrong but tried to console her the best way he could without saying too much about what was happening. He was at the hospital sitting next to Candis, waiting on her to wake up.

"I'm on my way, Dad," Ashley said.

"You sound upset, honey. You should probably go home and sleep it off."

"No Dad." Her voice was firm. She sped to the hospital, hoping that Candis was up because she needed those answers.

Her mind was racing: "Blood is suppose to be thicker than water, right? How the hell did this happen? How could she stoop so low? Oh my God, I hate her so much right now!" She started reflecting on the many times she and Campbell had been over to Candis's house, how many times Candis and Campbell had gone to the store together, how comfortable Campbell was around Candis. She always thought it was just brother-sister closeness. Who knew they were actually fucking?

"I'm such an idiot," she said aloud. How could she come to terms with the fact that her own sister was sleeping with her husband? Everything in her wanted to snap.

She soon arrived at the hospital, a tall white building with seven floors. It was the only hospital in town. She had many memories there; it's where she'd had her son and a miscarriage that she never disclosed to Campbell because he was out of town closing a major deal at the time. He had no idea how much she hurt.

She thought about the sacrifices she had made for him, putting her career on hold so that he could continue on his path of success. She was infuriated by the time she arrived on the seventh floor.

She walked in the room and ran up to her dad, who grabbed her and held her tight while she sobbed for her sister and the end of her relationship.

"Where's Campbell?" he asked gently. The thought made her cry harder.

After a few moments of consoling his daughter, her dad stepped out. He told her he needed to use the restroom, but he really needed to call Campbell.

"Son, where are you?" he said into the phone when he was a safe distance away.

"I'm working," Campbell said.

"Work can wait. Your wife needs you right now."

"I'll be on my way as soon as I can," Campbell mumbled.

"Make it quick." Ashley's dad hung up the phone and headed back to be with his daughters.

Ashley was so confused by her sisters's actions. She stood in front of her sister, getting more and more upset. Campbell continued to call Candis's phone, which made Ashley absolutely livid. She wanted them both dead. Then he texted her: "Baby, I'm sorry. I love you."

Ashley snapped. She calmly waited until everyone was gone and removed the oxygen tube from Candis's nose. Candis started gasping for air, opening her eyes at one point while her sister was standing over her. Ashley shed one tear at the thought of the sadness her sister had brought to her.

As Candis started to slip away, Ashley suddenly felt bad and put the oxygen tube back in her sister's nose. In a panic, she frantically tried to connect the other cables and monitors. But it was too late. Candis was gone.

Ashley sat in the corner and cried. She'd committed an unthinkable act in response to an unthinkable act. The nurses rushed in to try to revive Candis, but to no avail. In her distress, Ashley called Melvin. While she was on the phone, her dad came in the room and gave her the look that said, "What did you do?"

"I'll be right there," Melvin said on the other end of the line. He would drop everything without question to be with his friend. Ashley sent Campbell a text: "I hope you're happy. You killed my sister.

Ashley's dad called his wife to let her know what had happened to Candis. Jennifer arrived at the hospital in a matter of moments, or so it seemed to Ashley. Maybe she was just that out of it. Her father immediately took over talking with the hospital staff, familiarizing himself with what had taken his baby girl's life. He never once cried in front of Ashley; he knew he had to be strong for her. He ordered her to go home to rest and wondered aloud where the hell Campbell was and why wasn't he there for his wife, at least for appearances. He knew Campbell was a busy man, but no man could ever be too busy to tend to his wife at such a critical time. Besides, a lot of this stress rested on his shoulders. He made a mental note to look into that later.

In the following days, Ashley barely had to do anything for herself. Her dad's wife continued to prepare and bring meals over. Her best girlfriends came by to check on her. They split the day into shifts to sit with Ashley and man her house and cellphone. The phones were ringing off the hook, as expected. Old childhood friends, family members, and colleagues of both Ashley and Candis called to give their condolences.

Melvin wanted to respect Ashley and her marriage, and since no one else knew they were going through a divorce, he came by late in the evenings or early in the morning on his way to work to check on her.

Melvin and Ashley continued to see each other for months. He gave her enough space to get over her relationship and to work through the pain of losing her marriage and her sister. He helped her get her life back on track and started working with her on a modeling studio.

She wanted to mentor young women in the industry and felt this was the best way to give back.

She never spoke to Campbell again about anything that did not involve Cooper. She was completely done with him; he had lied to her for the last time. She was heartbroken by the deceit, and he was heartbroken by the loss of Candis, the love of his life.

They both masked the disdain they had for each other while raising their son.

They lived life.

About the Author

DAMOND DAVIS is an avid reader, writer, and traveller, who has covered the globe while experiencing his share of lived life. He grew up in Montgomery, Alabama, where many of the stories for the series took root. His undergraduate degree is from Austin Peay State University, and his graduate degree is from Webster University.

His calm demeanor and intellect have been a recipe for success. He serves his country with distinction and continues to find strength in doing something bigger than himself; he credits his subordinates and mentors for his success. He keeps kindness and empathy in the forefront of his mind, citing his grandmother (Helen Trawick) as his major source of inspiration.

Lived Life: The Counter Double Bluff is his first novel in the Lived Life Series, and he's very excited to get it out to the readers. He encourages open debate among readers.

He enjoys spending time with family and friends. Follow him on instagram at Montdavis7 and Twitter at DaMond Davis.